Step-Chain

All over the country children go to stay with step-parents, stepbrothers and stepsisters at the weekends. It's just like an endless chain. A step-chain. *Healing the Pain* is the tenth link in this step-chain.

I'm Ashley. I've got this pain. His name's Ben, he's Mum's boyfriend and he's totally in my face the whole time. Then there's Michelle, she keeps wanting to know how I'm getting on with him. I mean what's it got to do with *her*? She's not my friend. And suddenly I can't help thinking about the time Dad left Mum. I end up writing stuff down and find out that maybe I got a few things wrong . . .

Collect the links in the step-chain! You never know who you'll meet on the way . . .

Step-Chain

HEALING THE PAIN

Ann Bryant

EGMONT

First published in Great Britain 2003
by Egmont Books Limited
239 Kensington High Street
London W8 6SA

Copyright © 2003 Ann Bryant
Series conceived and created by Ann Bryant
Cover illustration copyright © 2003 Mark Oliver

The moral rights of the author and cover illustrator have
been asserted

Series editor: Anne Finnis

ISBN 1 4052 0432 X

3 5 7 9 10 8 6 4 2

Typeset by Avon DataSet Ltd, Bidford on Avon, B50 4JH
(www.avondataset.co.uk)
Printed and bound in Great Britain by
Cox & Wyman Ltd, Reading, Berkshire

CONTENTS

Step-Chain

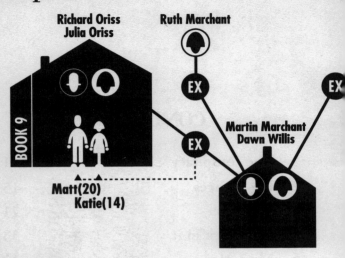

Richard Oriss
Julia Oriss

Ruth Marchant

EX

EX

BOOK 9

Martin Marchant
Dawn Willis

EX

Matt(20)
Katie(14)

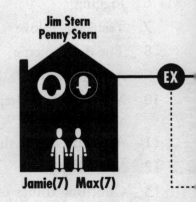

Jim Stern
Penny Stern

EX

Jamie(7) Max(7)

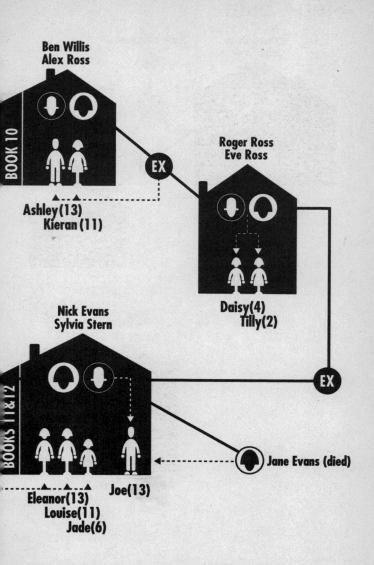

Ben Willis
Alex Ross

BOOK 10

Ashley(13)
Kieran(11)

EX

Roger Ross
Eve Ross

Daisy(4)
Tilly(2)

Nick Evans
Sylvia Stern

BOOKS 11&12

EX

Jane Evans (died)

Joe(13)

Eleanor(13)
Louise(11)
Jade(6)

Read on to discover all the links . . .

1 THE CONSPIRACY

Granny's loud voice cut in on my thoughts. 'I said do you want another cup of tea, Ashley?'

I dragged myself back to earth and shook my head. 'No thanks, Gran.'

She was giving me one of her searching looks. 'You're always daydreaming these days, young lady. Don't you get told off at school?'

I shrugged. 'Not really.'

The truth was I couldn't help daydreaming. There were so many horrible thoughts bugging me – thoughts about Ben, and when I'd first changed my mind about him. It was so brilliant at the beginning, when he and Mum started going out with each other. Mum stopped being tired and snappy all the time, and started being really good fun.

Kieran and I didn't actually see that much of her, because when she wasn't working at the hospital she was going out with Ben, but we weren't bothered because Mum was happy. Anyway, we'd got Granny. She'd been living with us for years – ever since Dad moved out.

But then gradually Mum and Ben stopped going *out* so much and started staying in together. And next thing we knew he was coming round here even when Mum was at work. I didn't mind at first, but after a while it got on my nerves, because he was always poking his nose into things that were nothing to do with him, and kept on asking us questions, like he was training to be a private eye or something. When he started trying to help with our homework, it really did my head in.

Thank God for Granny. She wouldn't dream of trying to help us with our homework. I looked at her, laughing at Kieran as he got revved up for one of his teacher impressions.

'Right, this is Mr Mercer, OK?'

Mr Mercer is *my* English teacher too. He's got the broadest Scottish accent known to man.

'Failing to plan,' said Kieran in a deep voice, marching dramatically over to Granny, and eyeballing her as though she was a bad student, 'is planning to *fail!*'

I couldn't help laughing. The accent was spot on, and Kieran had latched on to old Mercy's favourite catch phrase.

Granny started spluttering. 'That's quite clever, that is,' she said, repeating it to herself. 'Hmm . . . We could all learn something from that.' Then she looked at the clock and bit her lip.

The horrible thoughts came flooding back into my brain. I couldn't get away from them.

Something bad was about to happen. I could feel it. In fact, I'd been feeling it for days. Mum was building up to some big announcement, and I reckoned I knew exactly what it was going to be. I could have pumped Granny and got it out of her, because it was obvious she was in on the big conspiracy too. But I didn't, because I dreaded finding out I was right.

'When's Mum coming back?' asked Kieran, turning on the telly. He must have caught that glance at the clock too.

'She won't be long. Then I'm going to help Eileen with her jam-making.'

'You don't have to wait for Mum to get back, Gran. I don't mind babysitting Kieran.'

'I don't need babysitting. I'm eleven years old.'

Granny ignored me and flapped her hand at the telly. 'Can we turn it down a bit?'

'Sorry, Gran,' grinned Kieran. 'I thought you'd like it loud, now you're getting a bit deaf!'

'Less of that, young man.' She frowned at

the presenter on the pop channel that Kieran had on. 'Look at her! Fancy showing all that stomach when you're on telly!'

'Ssh!' said Kieran.

'I don't know why you watch such rubbish,' said Granny. 'Do another impression, go on.'

Kieran couldn't resist it. 'OK, I'll do Mr Carter.'

This was going to be interesting. Mr Carter is the games teacher and Kieran hates games. He's not very good at running and he's pretty uncoordinated so he isn't in any of the football teams at school. I feel sorry for him because it's obvious he really wishes he was good at football.

Our dad runs the line for the boys' match on Saturday afternoons, and whenever we go over to Dad's for the weekend, he tries to get Kieran to play. But he says things like, 'Puffed out already, Kieran? You've got to be fit to be any good at football, you know! You can learn a lot from just watching closely and listening to the coach . . .' I reckon poor old Kieran thinks that if he takes Dad's advice he might magically get really good at footie and go back and impress Mr Carter with his new skills.

Kieran's impression of Mr Carter wasn't bad. 'Come on, you lot! If you don't get a wriggle on, it'll be time to come in before we've even gone out!'

Granny chuckled. 'Your favourite subject, eh?'

Kieran rolled his eyes. 'Ought to be banned,' he said, turning back to the telly.

I waited till Granny had her back to me at the sink then crossed my fingers and asked if Ben was coming over.

'Huh! When *isn't* he coming over?' said Kieran sulkily.

Granny turned round with the dishcloth in her hand. 'Don't be like that. He's lovely, Ben is.'

And bang on cue, the back door opened and in he came, smiling away.

'Hello, everybody! And how are we all today?'

Kieran shot him a real evil. 'Where's Mum?'

'Hello, Ben,' said Granny pointedly, giving Kieran a *where are your manners?* look.

Ben smiled round and rubbed his hands together as though he was waiting for the Lottery result to be announced and he really fancied his chances. Then he pulled up a chair next to Kieran. 'Your mum's on her way. I thought I'd just drop by and see what you're all up to.'

Kieran mumbled that he was going to his room. Unfortunately he zapped off the telly at the same time, so that left me, Ben, Granny and an embarrassing silence.

'Is it still raining, Ben?' asked Granny.

Why didn't she look out of the window?

'Drizzling a bit. What did you have for tea, Ashley?' He was giving me the kind of encouraging smile you might give a three-year-old. Here we go . . .

I put the telly back on. 'Spaghetti.'

'Really! Do you know, when I was little I used to call spaghetti "basketti!"'

How interesting! 'I think I'll do my homework.'

He gave me a big beam. 'That's what I like to hear! Want any help?'

Granny brought a cup of tea to Ben. 'There you are, dear.'

'Cheers, Kath.'

'Word of advice, Ben,' she grinned. 'Never offer to help with homework.'

'OK, I know when I'm not wanted!'

Oh yeah? What are you doing here *then?*

I picked up my bag and followed Kieran's example.

Mum was late. I had nearly an hour to work myself up into a big temper. How dare Ben walk into our house like he owned the place and drive me and Kieran out of the kitchen. It was boring in my room, *and* cold.

So it was a relief in one way to hear the car pull up, but in another way I wished it never would, because I was dreading Mum making any big announcements. I left it a couple of minutes, so she and Ben could get the kissing bit over, then I went down.

'Hi, Mum.'

'Hi, love.' She looked a bit grim, but it might just have been a bad day at the hospital.

I thought I'd try delaying tactics. 'I've done my homework.'

'Good. Where's Kieran?'

Uh-oh! Something tells me this is not hospital grimness. 'Upstairs.'

'Right, I'm off to Eileen's,' said Granny. 'I said I'd give her a hand with her jam.'

Mum patted Granny's arm. 'She's lucky to have you, Mum.'

Granny didn't answer but a look passed between them as she went to call 'bye to Kieran upstairs.

'I'm off now, love! See you later.'

''Bye, Gran,' came the faint reply.

Ben drained his cup. 'I'll walk you to the corner, Kath. I'm going to get a bottle of wine from the shop.'

And there it was again – that same look. They must think I'm blind or stupid.

'Ashley, can you tell Kieran to come down, please?' Mum's voice sent a chill through me. 'I want a word with you both.'

'What about?'

She put on her *I'm trying to be patient* voice. 'I'll tell you when Kieran's here.'

So I went to the bottom of the stairs and yelled to him to come down, and by the time I went back into the kitchen Granny and Ben had gone. A minute later the three of us were sitting round the kitchen table.

Mum cleared her throat. 'You know I haven't been working nights at the hospital for ages now?'

'Yeah, so you can be with *him* in the evenings,' Kieran blurted out.

Mum hung on to her cool, but only just. 'His name is Ben, and that is not the reason.'

'What is then?'

'Because it's exhausting doing nights. I only did it when your dad first left because I needed the money so badly. But that's all history now. I should have packed it in years ago.'

Kieran grunted.

Mum took a deep breath. 'Anyway, I was going to say that now I'm not doing nights any more, there's really no need for Granny to carry on living here. She's got her own life.'

Inside I was getting colder and colder.

'You're so cruel!' shouted Kieran. 'She's just a poor old lady. You better not say you're chucking her out!'

'Well, it's not quite like that . . .'

'Yes it is!' Kieran's eyes were flashing like mad. I got a shock when he turned them on me. 'I'm right, aren't I, Ash? Tell her!'

I opened my mouth to agree with him, but Mum got in first. 'It was actually Granny's idea. She mentioned it a few weeks ago. The people renting her house are moving out, and she's keen to get back in there.'

I was speechless, so was Kieran. We just stared at Mum.

She started gabbling. 'Look, it's been lovely having Granny living with us . . .' My heart started to beat loudly. I knew what was coming. '. . . but we've got Ben now . . .'

Kieran looked daggers at Mum. 'You mean, *you've* got Ben now.'

He was saying everything I was feeling. I sat there. Numb. I'd known it was coming and yet I was so fazed I couldn't speak.

Mum lost her cool. 'No, I mean we've *all* got Ben now. He takes a great interest in you two.'

'Don't you get it? We don't *want* him taking an interest!' shouted Kieran.

'What's all this "we" business?' Mum snapped. 'Is this how you feel about Ben too, Ashley?'

Her eyes were boring into me. I gulped and tried to work out whether my reply could make any difference to what was about to happen. Maybe if I went carefully . . . 'He's OK . . .' Mum's shoulders dropped about ten centimetres, '. . . only I wish he didn't have to be round here all the time . . .'

Kieran nodded hard. 'Yeah, interfering with our homework and everything. It's nothing to do with him. He's not our dad!'

Mum bit her lip and looked at the table. There was a terrible silence.

'What?' I asked her in a whisper, knowing really.

She didn't answer.

'What?' said Kieran right into Mum's face.

She spoke very softly, her eyes going backwards and forwards from Kieran to me. 'I've been trying to find the right moment to talk to you both . . .'

Suddenly I couldn't bear it any more. 'If he moves in here, *I'll* move out.'

Kieran gasped and looked from me to Mum and back again.

Mum turned to brisk mode. 'Don't be silly, Ashley. I knew you'd react like this. Has either of you ever thought that I might want a proper partner again?' Her eyes were really flashing. 'Someone actually living in the house with me so I don't feel like a single mother?' Then she kind of slumped in her seat, as though her big announcement had taken it right out of her. I didn't care. Let her slump.

But a moment later she was sitting up again. 'So he's moving in at the weekend.'

'At the *weekend*!' My little brother had regained the power of speech.

And I had lost the will to live.

2 BIG CHANGES

The next day at school I told my best friend Luce the great news. It was break time and we were supposed to be outside, but it was freezing cold so we went into the toilets.

'I tell you, Luce, it was such a shock when she told me.'

'But you do quite like Ben, don't you?'

'He's OK in small doses, but I can't bear the thought of having him living in our house. Can you imagine all those questions the whole time? And he really winds me up with his goody-goody ways.'

'Poor you, Ash!'

'And it'll seem weird without Granny. She's lived with us for as long as I can remember.'

'You'll still see her though, won't you?'

'Yeah, she'll only be five minutes away. But *him* – he'll be there the whole time. Like a bad germ.'

'Won't he go out to work?'

'I wish.'

Luce looked puzzled, then she suddenly clicked. 'Oh yeah, he's a writer, isn't he?'

I curled my lip and nodded. 'Arty-farty stupid thing to be, isn't it?'

'I dunno. I think I'd be quite proud if I'd got a writer living in my house.'

'It'd help if I liked English, but I hate it. And it's going to be truly great, having to play music on the lowest volume known to man so I don't block His Lordship's creative channels.'

Luce gave me a sad smile and put her arm round me. 'Poor Ash,' she said again.

But then the sound of footsteps outside made us dive for the loos. We shut the doors then pressed the flush and a few seconds later we came out. That way, if a teacher was patrolling the place looking for people to send outside, she couldn't accuse us of loitering.

As it happened it was only Michelle Woods from our class. 'Berty's on the war path!' she said, pulling some make-up out of her pocket. She was talking about Miss Burton, the German teacher, who's not exactly the nicest teacher in the world.

'So anyway, Ben's moving in at the weekend, is he?' asked Luce as we picked up our bags.

I nodded and heaved a big sigh as I remembered something Mum had said. 'And guess what? He's having Granny's old room as his office.' I couldn't help sounding sarcastic. 'It's going to be a bundle of laughs with him around all day long tapping away at his latest novel.'

Luce put her hand on my arm. 'At least it's

quite a good job, being a writer, isn't it?'

'I'd rather he was a lighthouse keeper, to tell you the truth.'

Michelle stopped in the middle of putting her eye liner on. 'Poor you, Ashley.'

It was odd hearing her say that. She doesn't normally join in conversations with anyone. She's quite a loner at school, and out of school, she spends all her time down at the skateboard ramps with her brother and his mates. About a year ago she turned up at school with cuts and bruises on her face, and I heard her telling the teacher that she did it practising skateboarding down at the ramps. She must be getting better at it. I've not seen her with any bruises or anything for ages.

'Wh – what d'you mean?' I said.

'Poor you . . . with your new stepdad . . . and that.'

'He's not exactly a stepdad,' I said.

'So you don't like him?'

I didn't get why she was so interested, and I didn't really like talking about how I felt, except with Luce.

'He's OK,' I said, smiling rather shakily.

'Come on, Ash,' said Luce, 'we'd better get going before Bertie catches us.'

Michelle leaned forward and started putting mascara on. She wouldn't care *who* caught her.

It was Granny's last evening living with us. I went upstairs to see how she and Mum were getting on packing all her things. Just outside the bedroom door I stopped at the sound of Granny's voice.

'I'm only thinking about *you,* dear. You told me yourself that Ben should never have got married before, and I'm just worried about what you're getting yourself into here.'

Mum sounded as though she was nearly laughing. 'Oh come on, Mum, it's a bit late in the day to start worrying about me now.'

'I can't help it.' There was a pause, then Granny's voice went really soft. 'You know how awful it was when Roger walked out on you.'

'Oh Mum, that was Roger. This is Ben. He's not like that.'

'I don't see what the difference is. Ben walked out on his ex, didn't he?'

'No, it was a mutual decision to separate. As Ben says, he and Dawn should never have got married. They were both far too young.' Mum giggled. She was trying to lighten things up. 'And then Dawn went to the other extreme and married someone old enough to be her dad!'

I heard Granny laugh. 'All right then, dear. You've convinced me. Sorry to be an old mother hen!'

Huh! She might have convinced Granny, but no way was she *ever* going to convince me.

3 WHOOPS!

Kieran and I went to our dad's for the weekend. We don't have a regular routine or anything for going over there. Every so often Mum just suggests it. Sometimes it's a bit of a drag because I miss out on what Luce and my other friends are doing, but usually I'm fine with it.

Dad's partner's called Eve and they've got two little kids of their own – Tilly, who's two and Daisy, who's four. They're both really sweet. Eve loves me going over there, because I play with them lots and that gives her a break. But she hasn't always loved having me around.

Apparently, when I first started visiting I wouldn't speak to her *or* Dad and would only nod or shake my head. I was only little and I've got no memory of those days at all, so God knows what that was about.

On Saturday afternoon Kieran and Dad went off to the match as usual. While they were out Eve and I went shopping with Tilly and Daisy. We were first back and while Eve made tea I played with the kids.

Daisy clambered up on my lap and wound her arms tightly round my neck. 'I love you, Ashley,' she said.

'Well, don't strangle the poor girl then!' said Eve.

'When's Kieran and Daddy coming home, Mummy?'

'Any minute now, darling.' (She didn't realise how right she was.)

'Kiern! Kiern!' said little Tilly, tottering towards the back door.

Eve scooped her up and it was a good job she did because at that moment Kieran came crashing in at about a hundred miles an hour. He didn't even say hello, just went straight through to the hall, and seconds later we heard his clompy footsteps on the stairs. Uh-oh! Something had clearly rattled my dear brother's cage.

Dad came in just afterwards, looking pretty hacked off. He and Eve exchanged a look, then he sat down at the table and started cuddling Tilly.

'What's up with Kieran, Dad?'

'He had the chance of a game with the junior team because they were a player down, and the match was about to start.'

'But he didn't have any kit with him.'

Dad sighed. 'You sound exactly like him, Ashley. He came up with every excuse in the book, including feeling sick.'

Eve came to join us at the table. She looked

sympathetic. 'So did he play in the end?'

'Yep. It was Colin's boy, Liam, who couldn't go on because he'd sprained his ankle. Wow! I tell you, it took a bit of time persuading Kieran to play.'

'Poor lad,' said Eve. 'It was a bit cruel forcing him, if he really didn't want to play.'

That was exactly what I'd been thinking.

'It was Colin who persuaded him . . .'

'Did he do OK?' I asked quietly, thinking about Kieran's scowling face as he crashed through the kitchen.

'Well . . . not bad,' said Dad.

Eve and I waited. There was definitely something he hadn't told us yet. 'But they didn't win, and I think some of the lads gave him a bit of stick for being a bit . . . er . . . slow.'

I felt sorry for Kieran. It wasn't his fault if he'd let the side down. 'I'd hate it if I had to play netball in a team of girls I hardly knew.'

Dad looked a bit embarrassed.

'I'll go and have a quick chat with him, shall I?' said Eve.

But no sooner were the words out of her mouth than we all heard Daisy's loud voice yelling upstairs, 'I'll play football with you, Kieran. I like it slow.'

'Oh, terrific!' said Dad, rushing into the hall to grab Daisy. None of us had noticed that she'd gone out of the room.

'He'll never come down now,' I said quietly.

On Sunday morning Kieran woke up in a better mood. We all sat round having breakfast together while Tilly, who'd finished ages before, entertained us with her 'big girls' dancing' as she called it. It was the funniest thing I'd seen for ages. She'd obviously been watching how they dance in the girl bands on telly, because she sang at the top of her voice and jumped about all over the place with a huge smile on her face. Only her little legs weren't strong enough for all her big moves, so she kept on falling over, then getting up bottom first and carrying on as though nothing had happened.

Right in the middle of everyone laughing Daisy suddenly piped up, 'Is your Mummy's boyfriend at your house?'

'Eat your egg, Daisy!' said Eve a bit crossly.

'I expect so,' I answered. Out of the corner of my eye I could see Kieran scowling at his toast.

'Are they eating their breakfast too?' went on Daisy.

'If you're not going to eat your egg up, you won't get to go to the playroom at the pub later,' said Dad, trying desperately to shut Daisy up.

So Daisy crammed a massive forkful of scrambled egg in her mouth, then spat little bits of it out as she said, 'They might be having breakfast in their bed.'

'Daisy!' snapped Eve. 'Don't talk with your mouth full!'

Daisy did a big swallow then grinned at Eve.

'That's what you and Daddy did on Father's Day, didn't you?'

I couldn't get those words of Daisy's out of my head for the rest of the day. I'd always known that Mum and Ben would be sharing Mum's bedroom, so I wasn't sure what was making me feel so hacked off. But when Kieran and I were collecting our bags from upstairs, he suddenly said, 'If Ben thinks he's getting breakfast in bed on Father's Day, he can forget it. He's not our dad and he never will be.'

And that was when I realised which bit of Daisy's comment had got to me.

In Dad's car on the way back to our house, I remembered a book I'd once read, where a girl of about my age dreaded going back to her boarding school at the end of every school holiday, because she was really homesick. I felt like that, only in reverse. I wasn't homesick, I was just sick of home.

Dad must have been able to read my mind. 'I know you're not looking forward to living with a man about the place,' he said, sounding a bit embarrassed, 'but I'm sure you'll find it'll turn out better than you imagine.'

Kieran and I were silent, so he had another little go. 'I mean, you both get on all right with Ben, don't you? I've never heard you say anything against him.'

'He's OK,' I mumbled, because it was impossible to explain about Ben, except to Luce.

Kieran had a go though – and that got me revved up.

'He'd be all right if he'd stop asking us questions all the time –'

'Yeah, and treating us like babies –'

'And making us do our homework –'

'And interfering with our lives –'

I took a sideways glance at Dad. He was frowning. We all stayed quiet till we pulled up outside our place and got out of the car.

'Do you want me to come in?' Dad asked me gently.

I shook my head. The first time he asked that question was years ago and I went mad and refused to let him even get out of the car. I don't know why but I can't bear the thought of him being in the house with Mum. So he always sits in the car till I've gone into the house, then Kieran stands there waving him off.

'Give us a ring any time,' Dad went on, as he hugged us both. 'And don't worry. It'll be fine, I'm sure.'

Mum greeted us at the back door. 'Hello, you two! Had a good time?'

Kieran's eyes were darting round the kitchen as though he expected Ben to come climbing out of a cupboard at any second. 'Is he here?'

'Is *who* here?' asked Mum. She had her hands on her hips and it was pretty obvious she wasn't going to stand for any nonsense.

'Father Christmas! Who do you think?' said Kieran in a scathing voice.

I gasped. He wasn't usually this rude to Mum.

'Right, let's get something straight,' said Mum, wagging her finger at Kieran. 'All the time you are living under this roof I expect you to be polite to me and Ben. Nobody's asking you to call him Dad or anything like that, but he's *my* partner and the sooner you get used to the idea, the better it will be for all concerned. Got that?'

Then in walked Ben. 'Hello, guys! Had a good time?'

'OK,' said Kieran in a sulky voice.

'How were the nippers?' he asked me with his stupid bright smile.

'Fine.'

'And how was the match yesterday? Did you watch it?'

Kieran stared at the floor and didn't answer.

'We went to the pub at lunchtime today,' I

said quickly, to get the spotlight off Kieran.

'Which pub was that?' asked Ben.

Who cares which one it was. 'The Coach and Horses.'

'That's the one with the playroom, isn't it? Great fun for the nippers!'

Why did he have to make such a big deal of everything?

'Have you eaten since lunchtime?' Mum butted in – she could see that I was getting riled.

I shook my head.

She suddenly sounded as stupidly cheerful as Ben. 'Good, because we've got a lovely chicken casserole.'

Kieran looked up then, and didn't seem quite so hacked off, but personally I just felt embarrassed, listening to Mum playing at being Delia Smith.

'You two take your bags upstairs while I set the table,' said Ben, flinging open the cutlery drawer.

What! You think we're going to take orders from you!

Kieran picked up his bag, good as gold, and off he went. I guess he was concentrating on his stomach as usual.

That left me with a problem. If I'd gone hurrying off with my bag, same as Kieran, Ben might get the idea that it was fine for him to boss us around.

'Do you want any help, Mum?' I asked instead.

'No, we'll sort the meal out, thanks, love.'

I had a sudden cosy picture of Granny and me setting the table together. Now all of a sudden it's Ben. Well, I wasn't putting up with that.

'*I'll* set the table,' I said.

I had my back to both of them as I went to get out the plates, but I just knew they'd be exchanging a look. Good. They were getting the idea.

4 PUT A SOCK IN IT!

The next day, on the way home on the bus, I sat next to Luce. Two of our friends, Liz and Ella, were just in front of us. They knew about Ben, but not as much as Luce did.

'What's it like with *him* in the house, Ashley?' asked Liz.

I rolled my eyes. 'The pits.'

'Do you deliberately take ages in the bathroom, Ash? That's what I'd do,' giggled Ella.

I hadn't thought of that, but I made a mental note to make sure I did it from now on.

'He's not seriously going to be picking you

up from the bus after school, is he?' asked Luce.

'He'd better not! I couldn't believe it when he told Mum his wonderful idea. And Kieran went absolutely mad! I mean, Granny never did anything stupid like that.'

'I'm not surprised. You're not at primary.'

'Mum had the sense to tell him not to, thank goodness.'

'I bet that's a relief, isn't it?'

'You're not kidding!'

When Liz and Ella got off at the next stop, Michelle, who'd been sitting nearby, slid into their seat.

'So it's not going too well with your stepdad then, Ashley?'

I couldn't help feeling uncomfortable. It didn't seem right for Michelle to be talking like this. She's the girl who keeps herself to herself. Everyone knows that. And this was the second time she'd used *that* word. 'He's not my stepdad, OK?'

'What is he then? Just some bloke your Mum picked up?'

I thought she was being horrible at first, but then I realised it was a perfectly genuine question.

'He's . . . he's not anything.'

'Yeah, right.'

She turned back round and I felt stupid for giving such a pathetic answer.

Luce and I looked at each other. If we hadn't been right behind Michelle we would have had a whispered conversation together, trying to work out why she was so interested in the subject of Ben. But she might have heard us, so we kept quiet. I don't know what Luce was thinking about, but personally I was getting myself all wound up in case Ben had decided to ignore Mum and come and meet us at the bus stop anyway. I turned round and saw Kieran at the back with his mates. He was standing up so he could see more out of the window. His eyes were darting all over the place. He must have had the same thought as me.

The bus pulled up at our stop. No sign of Ben. I let my breath out. 'See you tomorrow, Luce. 'Bye, Michelle.'

'Good,' said Kieran, jumping off the bus after me, 'I don't have to answer any stupid questions like, "How are you guys doing? What was school like? Had any tests or anything?" Doesn't he realise we think he's stupid?'

I was about to answer when I noticed someone rushing towards us. Omigod!

'Sorry, I lost track of the time. How are you guys doing?'

Behind us the bus was pulling away. I glanced up to see Luce's sympathetic eyes watching me through the window. Michelle wasn't looking, thank goodness.

'I thought Mum said you didn't have to come and meet us. I *am* thirteen, you know.'

'Yes!' said Kieran aggressively.

Ben smiled. *Didn't he* ever *have bad moods?* 'I know I don't *have* to – I just felt like a walk.' He laughed. 'I found I was beginning to see double, staring at that computer screen.'

We walked in silence for a moment. Kieran and I were determined not to make conversation, then maybe Ben would get the message and stay at home next time.

'So, what was the best part of today?' *Oh, please!* 'Ashley – you first.'

'Dunno,' I mumbled.

'Kieran?'

'Nothing.'

'Well, the best part of *my* day was first thing this morning. Did you know that our brains work better in the morning?'

Neither of us replied.

'I expect you have to do maths and English and things like that at the beginning of the school day, don't you?'

'Depends what your timetable is,' said Kieran.

'The whole school can't do maths, can they?'

'Good point,' said Ben. 'I suppose by secondary school all subjects are just as hard work – apart from games, that is. Games takes place in the afternoon, doesn't it?'

'Mm,' I said, which was all I could manage.

'So did you have games today, either of you?'

Why didn't he put a sock in it?

'No.'

'What about you, Kieran?'

'Yes.'

'What did you do? Football?'

'Mm.'

'That's another thing the brain needs – fresh air. Oxygen. All that running around will have done you good.'

'I hate it,' Kieran informed him.

Ben didn't say anything. I glanced at him. He was frowning at the ground.

For the next few minutes till we got home, he tried asking us about all sorts of schooly things, but we just grunted one-word answers, so eventually he gave up.

Normally, Granny would let us in the kitchen then go straight to the kettle and switch it on. While the water was boiling she'd get a few buns from the pantry and put them on a plate. *Here you go, loves. A bit of home baking. How about that!*

Kieran went to the cupboard, took three biscuits out of the tin and started jamming them in his mouth.

Ben didn't look very pleased as he got a plate out of the cupboard and handed it to Kieran. 'You don't want to get crumbs on the floor, do you?'

Kieran took the plate but didn't reply.

I was feeling irritated because I was starving hungry and I wanted to grab some biscuits too. Trouble was, if I got myself a plate, it would look as though I was cooperating. On the other hand, if I didn't, he'd think I was just being bolshie and he might report back to Mum. I wasn't about to give Mum anything that she could hold over us as being our fault, not Ben's. That would just be playing into his hands.

'Granny usually made buns or a cake,' I said, without looking at him, as I got out a plate.

'Oh dear, I don't know if I can live up to such high standards, but then again, I could always give it a whirl!'

Kieran was heading out of the kitchen.

'Have you got any homework, Kieran?'

'No.' He didn't even turn round.

'What about you, Ashley?'

'A bit.'

'What subject?'

Get off my case, will you?

'Granny never asked all these questions. She trusted us to do our homework, and let us do it when we felt like it.'

He turned and put the kettle on. 'I was just taking an interest, Ashley. That's all.'

Yeah? Well, don't!

5 MEMORIES

I raced downstairs when I heard Mum's front door key in the lock, because I was determined to get to her before Ben did. 'Hi, Mum! Did you have a nice day?'

'You took the words right out of my mouth!' Ben remarked.

Mum broke into a rapturous smile at the sound of Lover Boy's voice.

'What a lovely greeting!' She kissed me. 'Yes, thank you, love.' Then she kissed him. I didn't watch. 'Where's Kieran?'

'Upstairs. He's been up there since we got

home from school.' I wanted to leave her in no doubt that our space was being badly invaded. 'So have I.'

I might as well not have spoken for all the notice Mum took. 'Mmm! Lovely smell.'

Ben smiled at her, then tried to get me in the smile too. 'I thought I'd give you a nice surprise and cook something ambitious for once.'

'Brilliant! I'm starving!' said Mum.

Kieran and I didn't say much during the meal, but Mum and Ben prattled on, mainly talking about the hospital. Mum was telling us about a seventeen-year-old who'd been in a motorbike accident. Every so often she doles out the 'let's-put-Kieran-off-ever-having-a-motorbike' lecture. The injuries did sound awful, though. As I listened to her, I found myself remembering that Ben had been in a hospital bed when Mum had first met him. It seems like ages ago but it was only about a year. Mum had never told me what he was actually in hospital for and I wasn't all that interested anyway. Back then I never thought she and Ben would finish up living together, did I? I was quite curious now though, but there was no way was I was going to ask. That would be showing far too much interest.

At the end of the meal, Ben suddenly said, 'It's a lovely evening. Who wants a walk?'

A walk! In the dark? When we could be watching TV? Which planet did he come from?

'I'll clear the table,' said Mum. 'Why don't you two go with Ben?'

Kieran looked as though she'd suggested we clean the toilet.

'I've got homework,' I mumbled.

'I thought you did that earlier when you were in your room,' said Ben.

He was right – I did. As fast as possible because I'm not very good at English, so I only ever do the shortest essay I can get away with, then there's less to be criticised by Mercy.

'I didn't finish it.'

'What subject?'

'English.'

'Oh, I'd be interested to see that!' He grinned.

I closed my eyes and opened them again slowly.

'What about you, Kieran?' asked Mum.

'Got homework an' all,' he mumbled, heading for the door.

Mum was playing it tough. 'Well, you can help me clear away first.'

Kieran sighed an over-the-top sigh, grabbed his plate and marched over to the dishwasher.

'I thought you said you didn't have any homework when I asked earlier on,' Ben pointed out.

'I forgot, OK?'

Ben ignored the sneery expression on Kieran's face. 'Well, why don't you come and have a walk now – or a jog, even better – then I'll help you with whatever it is when we get back. Remember what I told you about oxygen to the brain?'

'I don't want to.' Kieran shut the dishwasher as noisily as possible, then swung round.

Mum stopped him in his tracks by gripping him by the shoulders. 'Go on, off you go. Just for ten minutes.'

'No, Mum! I want to watch telly.'

'I thought you had homework to do.'

'*And* that.'

'OK,' said Ben. 'Bring the homework down here and I'll give you a hand.' Kieran gave Mum a withering look.

'Your choice,' she said brightly. 'Either go for a jog or go and get your homework.'

Kieran went out and slammed the door behind him.

Mum looked at Ben. Ben shook his head.

'Go and get your English,' said Mum quietly to me.

It would have been childish if I'd slammed the door too, so I settled for a glare.

* * *

'So did he help you both with your homework?' Luce was sitting on the desk with her feet on the chair, leaning forwards, all wide-eyed.

'He looked at the pathetic English essay I'd written and said he thought it was good. I knew he was lying because I'm rubbish at English. Then he read the title out loud all slowly and thoughtfully, like this –' I put on the nearest I could get to Ben's irritating voice – '"*IT'S ALL MY FAULT . . .*" Then he asked me what was the very first thing that came into my head when I thought about the title. I said, "Nothing" and he just kept looking at me, so in the end I had to say something just to get his eyes off me, so I said, "A dolls' picnic."'

'Was it true?'

'Yeah, it was true OK.' I giggled. 'It didn't have anything to do with the title, mind you, but it was true.'

Luce giggled too. 'I bet he didn't know what to say then, did he?'

My mind scanned back over all the questions he'd asked me.

'*When did the picnic take place?*'

'*Years ago.*'

'*Were* you *there on the picnic?*'

'*Yeah.*'

'*How did you feel?*'

'*I dunno. I was only little when I used to take my dolls outside to play at picnics. I've no idea why the title just happened to remind me of that.*'

'Oh, he knew what to say all right.'

Luce was leaning so far forwards, I thought she was going to fall off her desk. 'Go on, then . . .'

'Well, God knows why, but he thought it was some kind of brilliant connection I'd made and he said it would be really cool if I re-wrote the whole essay and made it all about that dolls' picnic and said exactly how I felt when I was a little girl. I told him no way was I going to go to all that trouble because I didn't want Mercy

Features taking the rip out of me in front of the whole class, and he just said, "Hmmm". Then he told me about when he was my age and something like that had happened to him.'

'Yeah?'

'And next he picked one paragraph and said I could work the picnic – just briefly – into that bit. So I did a few sentences just to shut him up. And at least it made the essay a bit longer. Anyway, he read my new bit and said it was really good, but it'd be even better if I brought my feelings into it more. So I told him I didn't know what he was on about, and said I was off to bed.'

Luce's eyes were still big. 'Did he help Kieran too?'

'Dunno. I heard a bit of shouting when I was in my room, so I suppose he must have tried, but I don't expect he got very far.'

'Talking about your stepdad, are you?' Michelle had appeared from nowhere.

She was really beginning to bug me now. For a moment I forgot she was quite scary. 'He's not my stepdad, I've told you!'

'Don't blame you for being mad. Is it really pants?'

I wished she wouldn't keep on asking me stuff about Ben. I don't mind talking to Luce, or even a few of my other friends, about him, but it makes you feel like the saddest person in the class if everyone knows you're having a dodgy time at home and there's nothing you can do about it.

'He's OK,' I said, trying to smile.

'Yeah. Right.'

She seemed to be waiting for me to say something else, but I didn't. Then the bell rang for the end of break, so we both went to get the stuff we needed. It was English next. I pulled my essay out of my bag, and as my eye fell on the paragraph about the dolls' picnic, I thought back to last night . . .

After I'd gone to bed, I'd stayed awake for ages thinking about that picnic. The memories had been churning away inside my head, and in the end I'd got out of bed and sat at my desk. Then before I'd known what I was doing, I'd started to write . . .

It was like I was four years old again and I could remember all the dolls' faces and what clothes they had on and everything. I'd been the mother to the dolls and I'd known exactly what each doll's character was like. Miranda Doll was the shy one, Keely Doll (don't know where that name came from!) *the naughty one, Alice Doll the one who kept wanting to hide* (I used to love sitting her in low branches of trees and deep inside leafy shrubs). *And then there were the scruffy triplet dolls that I'd bought at a jumble sale. They were the sick babies, who only had one set of clothes to share between all three of them, so they always had to have a cover over them.*

One day I'd wanted to give them a picnic and Mum had said she thought I ought to have an inside picnic, but I'd got cross and said that it wouldn't be a proper one unless it was outside. Then she got cross so I waited till she wasn't looking, sneaked outside and set everything out on an old blanket that used to be in my cot. In front of each doll I'd put a little plastic plate with bits of grass on it, and leaves and moss and gravel and anything else that I could find which I could pretend was food. Then I'd looked up at the sky and wondered if it was going to rain . . .

My memories were coming so fast by this point that my pen could hardly keep up with them. I'd been scribbling away for ages, but I suddenly stopped and thought how stupid it was, a thirteen-year-old writing about a dolls' picnic that she'd had when she'd been four. Stupid and pathetic. And to think Ben had wanted me to write my whole essay on this babyish subject! He didn't know what he was talking about. He might be a writer, but he wasn't an English teacher.

I chucked the pages in my drawer and went back to bed.

And now I was walking down the school corridor, heading for another boring English lesson, and all those memories seemed a million miles away – like it had been someone else scribbling in the middle of the night.

6 JOGGING

After school I sat on the bus with Luce, feeling really tense.

'Do you think he'll be waiting for you, Ash?'

'Not if he's got any sense. Kieran says he's definitely going to stay on the bus if *he's* there.'

As usual Michelle was tuning in, even though she was sitting across the aisle and three seats back. 'Hasn't he got a job, then?'

I didn't want people to think Mum was living with a loser, but then I didn't want to say what Ben's job was. Something told me Michelle would take the rip out of me about that.

'He works from home.'

'Oh yeah, you said. He's a writer, isn't he?'

I closed my eyes and looked out of the window, but Michelle didn't get the hint. 'What kind of stuff does he write?'

'Novels.'

'Yeah? Have you read any?'

I shook my head. I didn't have a clue what kind of novels Ben wrote except that they were for adults, not children or teenagers, because Mum said *she* liked them.

Michelle left me alone after that, thank goodness, and as I stared out of the window I tried to puzzle out why she was so interested in Ben. Maybe she'd got a stepdad too. *Stepdad! Why am I calling Ben a stepdad?*

I nearly asked Michelle outright, but she'd only start asking me more questions about Ben, so I nudged Luce, who had her nose in a magazine. 'Has Michelle got a stepdad?' I mouthed.

She shrugged. 'Dunno. Never asked. I'll find out from my brother if you want. Michelle's brother's in his class.'

'OK.'

Kieran and I got off at our stop. There was no sign of Ben, thank God. All the way home I felt as though I was holding my breath, half expecting him to suddenly appear at any second. I'd actually got my hand on the door handle when his voice made Kieran and me jump. 'Hi, you guys!' We turned to see him poking at a pile of black ashes with a stick. I couldn't help being curious. Making bonfires in the back garden wasn't a thing we'd ever done before. Mum always said the garden was too small.

'What have you been burning?'

'My first draft. It's a little ritual of mine.'

'He means the kind of rough copy of his book,' I whispered to Kieran.

Kieran wasn't impressed. He pushed the

back door open. 'I couldn't care if he's been burning his underpants.'

Normally I would have found that quite a witty comment, but I was too curious about Ben doing this ritual thing to react. 'Don't you need your first draft any more? I mean, to copy from . . .?' I felt stupid as soon as I'd spoken. 'Oh no . . . You've got it on the computer, haven't you?'

He poked and stabbed at the middle of the ashes, where bits of white charred paper hadn't quite burnt away. 'No, it's not even saved on the computer, because I do my corrections on the first draft to turn it into the second one. But you're right, I ought to keep this hard copy just in case I want to change anything back to how it was. I just get to a point when I know I don't need it any more, so I burn it. It's all stupid psychology – but then that's what ninety per cent of writing is.'

I didn't mind it when he talked like this –

about himself, not me. I wandered over and stared at the ashes, which glinted and sparked as the stick stirred them round. I've always been drawn to fire. I found it hard to drag my eyes away from the flames, even when they'd died down to nothing more than a glow, so it gave me a shock when Kieran suddenly called out, 'I need some of that sticky-back stuff from the stationery shop. We've got to have our science text books covered by tomorrow.'

Kieran had spoken quite aggressively. I glanced at Ben, wondering how he'd react.

He left it a couple of beats then said, 'OK, I'll walk into town with you. I could do with the exercise.'

I know my brother and I reckon he was hoping Ben would offer to go into town for him. 'I'll miss all the good telly if I go now,' he whined.

'The shops'll be shut if you go any later,' Ben pointed out. He was already heading for the house. 'If we jog down, we'll be back in no time. I'll just get some money. Hang on.'

Kieran came and joined me at the bonfire. He was scowling as he kicked the ground. 'Why doesn't he go on his own? *I'm* not jogging anywhere. I'll feel stupid.'

I didn't get the chance to reply because Ben was coming out of the house. 'Will you be OK on your own for half an hour, Ashley?'

I nodded without looking up. 'Fine.'

The fire was like a magnet. I couldn't get my eyes off it. As I stared I found myself thinking about the dolls' picnic again. I had the sudden urge to see if I could find any old photos of my dolls.

There were four photo albums in the cupboard, each one with an index at the back. I sat at the kitchen table and turned the pages slowly, but there wasn't a single one of my dolls, and neither were there any photos of me above the age of eleven and yet I knew plenty had been taken. Mum obviously hadn't got round to putting them in the album yet. I turned the whole cupboard out on to the floor and sure enough, there were loads of recent photos of me and Kieran amongst the clutter.

I left them in a pile on one side then started putting everything else back neatly in the cupboard. A few minutes later the back door was pushed open and in came Ben and Kieran, puffing and sweating. They'd been so quick. I was about to crack a joke about training for the Olympics but the look on Kieran's face made me change my mind. I'd never seen him look so hot and bothered. He poured out a glass of water, gulped it down and went stomping off.

Ben didn't seem to be taking any notice. He nodded at the cupboard. 'Looking for anything in particular, Ashley?'

What had it got to do with him? 'No.'

I was expecting more questions but he just

started humming to himself as he made the tea and put some biscuits on a plate.

Poor old Kieran. I mean, Ben couldn't have forced him to jog, could he? But I might get my head snapped off if I went anywhere near Kieran to ask, so I decided to stick with the photos. I'd spread them out all over the kitchen table in rows according to when they were taken, and now I wished we had a spare album to stick them in.

Ben peered over my shoulder. 'They'd look good in a big collage, wouldn't they?'

'How do you mean?'

'You know – in one of those clip frames, like the one that's halfway up the stairs.'

He'd actually had quite a good idea for once. I rushed off to get it. 'I'm sure Mum doesn't want to keep this old picture in here. It's been there for ages. I'll swap it for these photos. She'll be really pleased.'

'Wait until she gets back, eh? Just in case

she's got a particular soft spot for the picture. You never know.'

I do know, actually, because I've been living with her all my life, so I know her better than you.

'But then it won't be a surprise.'

'Well, why don't I ask her about it subtly this evening, then you can do the collage tomorrow, as long as she doesn't mind.'

He was really making me mad. It was nothing to do with him what I did in my own house, and I wanted to do it there and then. 'She definitely won't mind,' I said, starting to take the clips off the frame.

His strict tone of voice took me back. 'Ashley, I think you should wait. If you want to give your mum a surprise, why don't you get your homework out of the way now, then you'll be free to help clear away the meal later.'

The words were out of my mouth before I could stop them. 'And why don't you mind your own business!'

He didn't say a thing as I angrily swept the photos off the table on to the floor and ran out of the room with my school bag.

Kieran was in the sitting room, watching telly. 'I heard you yelling. What happened?'

I flopped on the settee and answered in a disgusted tone. 'His Royal Highness didn't think I ought to take the picture out of that glass thing halfway up the stairs until I'd asked Mum's permission, and he also thought I ought to get my homework done so I could help later.'

Now I actually put it into words it didn't sound as bad as it had seemed a minute ago.

Kieran obviously didn't think so either. 'That's nothing. He kidded me that it was later than it really was to make me jog faster so I wouldn't miss my programme. Then he told me the real time when we were home. I'd still got ten minutes to go. He thought it was a great joke, ha ha!'

I couldn't help a giggle escaping. 'He *didn't*!

Are you sure you're not exaggerating?'

Whoops! Wrong, Ashley.

'No, I am *not* exaggerating. And it's not funny either. Anyway, you can shut up – I'm trying to watch this.'

So I went back into the kitchen to make a cup of tea. It was a bit embarrassing but I wasn't going to let Ben stop me from going into my own kitchen. I planned to ignore him whatever he said.

Surprise, surprise, he'd made me one and left it on the table. He'd also picked up all the photos. I took a sip of the tea, then informed him in my hardest voice that I couldn't do my homework until Mum got back because it was biology and she could help me with the answers.

Actually, I didn't have any intention of asking Mum. It wasn't even written homework. It was just learning for a test, and knowing our biology teacher we wouldn't get the results for weeks anyway. But if it *had* been written, I'd never have asked Mum for help. It's much less hassle to just copy it from one of the brainy ones at school the next day. The trouble with involving grown-ups in homework is that they always go into so much detail and make you look things up and copy it all out neatly and stuff like that.

'You're right,' he said with a little chuckle. 'There's not a lot your mum doesn't know about biology. What is it?'

'What do you mean?'

'What aspect of biology?'

I couldn't remember so I chucked the text book on the table, said 'We've got a test, page 34,' and went off with my tea.

When I came back later he'd done a big diagram of the circulation of the blood. 'This takes me back,' he smiled. 'I can still remember how I learnt this when I was at school. I've got the most terrible memory so I have to find my own way of memorising things.'

'Terrible memory?' I couldn't help being curious. I'd got one too.

'Do you want me to show you?'

I sat down and pulled my face into an expression of *I suppose I'll have to put up with it, but don't think I'm interested because I'm not.*

And fifteen minutes later I reckon I understood everything there was to know about the circulation of the blood *and* I could do the diagram by heart.

I did a kind of grunt that might have been a thank you, because anything more than that would have been sucking up to him.

7 TEENAGER IN LOVE

Kieran was on some kind of high. We were walking home from the bus stop a few days after the biology homework day, and he couldn't stop talking about the games lesson.

'Mr Carter said I was moving round the pitch much more quickly. He kept on calling out, 'Well done, Kieran!'

'Why?'

'Because I *was* doing well. Why d'you think?'

'Yeah? How come?'

He looked a bit sheepish. 'Well, you know when Ben made me run back from the stationery shop . . .'

'Yeah.'

'Well, when I was going on about how puffed I was, he said I wouldn't be puffed the next time. At first I ignored him because I was mad with him, but then he said that when he was a boy he hated games lessons until one day, they had a different teacher and he made Ben realise it was all to do with fitness. And Ben started jogging – you know, training – and it worked.'

It seemed odd imagining Ben telling Kieran all this stuff. He'd obviously had quite an effect on my little brother.

'And yesterday,' Kieran went on, all excited, 'after school when you went to Luce's I thought I'd just see if he was talking rubbish or not, so when I got home I ran up and downstairs for ages, and it was incredible because I *did* feel fitter. Then today, after lunch, me and Jonno jogged round the pitch four times and –'

'Yeah, OK, I think I've got the idea.' *Poor disillusioned boy thinks he's ready to play for England.*

'Yeah, but guess what? Mr Carter wants me to play in the second team in the match against Langton Woodville! And . . .'

There's more?

'. . . I'm going to see if I can get another game when I'm at Dad's. Then I'll show 'em!'

When we got home we found Ben gardening. He'd mown the lawn and done a load of weeding. He was right in the middle of pulling out a massive plant when we appeared.

'Hi, you guys! Just in time. Give us a hand, can you? I'm not letting this old thing defeat me!'

'What is it?' I asked.

'Does Mum mind you pulling her stuff out?' asked Kieran accusingly.

'It's a bramble, and no she doesn't mind. OK, one of you get that spade and try and lever it out from behind. And the other one hold on to me. I haven't got the strength on my own.'

The moment the word 'strength' was mentioned, Kieran was sold. Now he'd cracked the jogging I suppose he thought he'd demonstrate how strong he was. He put his arms round Ben's waist and stood there, face all tense and determined, like he was about to do a tug-of-war. That left me on spade duty. I wasn't sure if I'd be much good at this, but I picked the spade up and jammed it in the ground. Then I put my foot hard down on it to try and shift the root a bit. After a few seconds it began to move.

Ben sounded excited. 'OK, Kieran, on the count of three. One . . . two . . . *three!*'

The massive bramble root came out as Kieran and Ben toppled backwards and my spade shot a great spray of soil all over my face and my school uniform.

'Geronimo!' cried Ben as he leapt to his feet and gave Kieran a hand up. Then they both saw the state of me and cracked up laughing.

I was furious. 'I've got soil in my mouth, you know! And look at my uniform. Mum'll go spare.'

'Sorry, Ashley,' spluttered Ben. 'I know we shouldn't laugh. He turned to Kieran, who was still chuckling a bit. 'Well done, mate. You're pretty strong for your age, aren't you?'

I could tell Kieran was proud of himself. It was the first time I'd seen him give Ben anything resembling a nice look since he'd moved in with us. 'I'll give you an arm wrestle later if you want.'

'I won't stand a chance!' laughed Ben.

Glad you're having fun, boys, but what about me? I coughed as though I was choking – which I wasn't – and started brushing myself down. Then I realised that the handle of the spade was all dirty and I'd smeared a horrible greeny-black colour right down my skirt. I rubbed at it, but it only made it worse.

'Uh-oh! My fault!' said Ben. 'We need some stain remover. Do you know if there's anything like that in the house, Ashley?'

I shook my head. Mum wasn't the kind of organised mother who bought things like stain remover.

'Do us a favour, Kieran,' said Ben. 'You're faster than me at jogging. Can you get down to the hardware shop and ask if they've got anything? Explain what it's for. Here, take this.' He pulled a few coins out of his pocket.

Talk about sucking up. Kieran kind of swayed from foot to foot and went a bit pink at the tops of his cheeks. He was obviously dead chuffed because Ben thinks he's strong and faster at jogging than him. Huh! It'd take more than a couple of pathetic compliments to get round me!

As Kieran ran off, I watched Ben tidying away the garden things. I wanted to ask him about that clip frame, but if I struck up a conversation he might think I'd forgiven him for laughing at me. And I hadn't. No way.

I tried to sound as sullen as possible. 'Did you ask Mum about that picture in the clip frame?'

'Yes, and it's not a particular favourite of hers.'

I could have told you that. 'You didn't mention what I'm planning to do with it, did you?'

'No, don't worry, I gave nothing away.'

'Good!' I made for the back door.

'Oh, Ashley . . .'

'Yeah?'

'Homework first. It's a good habit to get into.'

I couldn't believe my ears. Just when I thought he might be lightening up a bit, and wasn't going to mention it, he'd gone and spoilt it all.

'Mum lets me do my homework when I like, actually.'

'Well, we've had a chat, your mum and I, and she's quite happy for me to supervise homework and the like. It's difficult for her, when she works so hard . . . So it'll be me signing your homework record from now on!' He was grinning away, as though I'd be pleased with their wonderful plan.

My blood was boiling. 'It's supposed to be a *parent* signing your homework record.' Then I stormed into the house and went straight up to my room.

I sat on the bed seething. No way was I going to let *him* sign it. He wasn't even a grandparent. That was an idea – I'd go round and see Granny. And I wouldn't ask *his* permission either. I'd just go.

'Hello, love. What a nice surprise!'

I hugged her and thought how lovely it was to see her smiling face. But something was missing from her little house and I couldn't think what it was at first. I looked round the kitchen.

Granny chuckled. 'What have you lost?'

'Nothing. I was just wondering . . .'

'Sorry I can't offer you a cake or anything, but I think I can scrape up a couple of biscuits.'

That's what it was – the smell. I kind of associated Granny with baking smells.

'It's OK, I'm not hungry. I just wanted to get away from *him*.'

'Oh dear . . . What's he done now?'

We sat down at the table and I told Granny about the homework record. 'It's supposed to be for parents to sign, and he's not even our dad or anything.'

She left it a couple of beats then said, 'It's probably all for the best that he's got his finger on the pulse, love. You're lucky to have someone to help you, you know.'

I opened my mouth to put her straight, to explain that I don't want his help, but then I remembered the biology test we'd had that day. For the first time in my life I'd found it quite easy because I'd actually been able to remember the whole circulation of the blood, using

Ben's methods. 'Well . . . yeah, but . . .'

Granny nodding approvingly. 'I bet he knows a fair bit, doesn't he, being a writer?'

'He's useless at cooking . . . and he's not very strong either. He couldn't even pull a bramble out without me and Kieran helping.'

While I'd been talking I'd noticed Granny glancing at the clock a few times. 'Were you going to watch something on telly, Gran?'

'What? Oh no . . . I don't get much time for telly these days.'

'Because of sorting the house out, you mean?'

'Well, that . . . and because of people popping round to see me.' Her eyes drifted to the clock again.

'Are you expecting someone now?'

She looked a bit guilty. 'What me? No . . . not specially.' She jumped up and started clearing things away. Then she suddenly gave me an anxious look. 'They do know you're here, don't they, your mum and Ben?'

Now it was my turn to look guilty. 'Mum's not back yet . . .'

'But you told Ben you were coming here, didn't you?'

'Er . . . not exactly.'

'Oh my goodness! He'll be tearing his hair out, wondering where you are.'

'No he won't. He'll think I'm still in my room. I nipped out the front way.'

'Well, all the same, you'd better be getting back, love.'

'You could ring him if you want.'

'Yes, and . . .'

The front door bell went.

I don't believe this! He's actually come round here to look for me!

Granny glanced at herself in the mirror above the telephone table and fluffed up her hair, then practically skipped away to answer the door. She was all pink when she came back in the kitchen. A man with bushy eyebrows and a very tanned face followed her in. I just stared.

'This is Sidney Eliott,' said Granny.

Sidney approached me, his hand outstretched. 'Hello, young lady. I've heard a lot about you.' He must have wondered why I was speechless with my jaw hanging open. 'Only good things, I can assure you!'

Granny giggled like a teenager in love.

Suddenly I wished I'd stayed at home.

8 THE DOLLS' PICNIC

I set off for home very slowly, kicking stones as I went, and not caring that I was scuffing my shoes. It was bad enough having a *mum* with a boyfriend, but a granny too? Spare me!

She said she'd phone Ben in case he was worrying. Let's hope he was. Then maybe he'd think twice about expecting me to obey his stupid rules.

'Hiya!'

I looked up to see Kieran running towards me in his full PE kit and a sweatband round his head. (What did he think he looked like?)

I spoke in my most sarcastic voice. 'Well, look who it is! The famous middle distance runner, Kieran Ross!'

'You're for it,' was all he said.

I glanced behind him and sure enough, there was Ben in the distance, jogging towards us

'Ashley,' he said, trying to catch his breath, 'I don't want you going off like that again. Your mum's in a complete state.

'Is she home?'

'No, I rang her at the hospital.'

'What'd you do that for?'

'To see if she had any idea where you might have gone.'

'It doesn't exactly take Albert Einstein to work it out,' I muttered under my breath as I carried on walking.

Unfortunately, he heard. And he didn't sound too happy. 'It might seem obvious to you, but it wasn't to me. I'm in charge of you until your mum gets home, and I was frantic with worry.'

'I'll carry on for a bit now we've found her, Ben,' said Kieran, jogging off.

'OK, mate. Just go as far as Gran's and I'll see you back at home. Then I'll give you that arm wrestle you were talking about.'

'Cool!'

What was with all this sudden chummy politeness?

Mum had a go at me the moment she walked through the door. 'I don't know what you think you're playing at, Ashley, but you'd better think again, because I'm not having this kind of behaviour!'

I wanted to ask what she was going to do about it, but I didn't quite dare. Her eyes were really blazing. God knows why I ever thought of making her that collage. She didn't deserve any presents from me.

'Have you done your homework?'

'We haven't got any.'

Kieran came crashing in from the other room. 'Hi, Mum!' Then he got down into the press-up position. 'Hey, Ben, watch this! I can do three!'

'Hang on a sec, son.'

That did it. That word. It made me snap.

'He's not your "son". And I'm not your daughter. We've got a perfectly good dad of our own. Why don't you just butt out!'

Mum turned all her anger on me. 'Ashley!'

'It's all right, Alex,' said Ben. 'It was my fault. I shouldn't have used that word. I wasn't thinking.'

He smiled round at everyone, and I felt like throwing up.

'I'm going to tidy my room.' It was a pathetic exit line, but who cared?

My bedroom was directly above the kitchen. I lay on my bed, listening to those three talking and laughing together. Kieran was such a traitor. He was acting like Ben's number one fan – and all because Ben had got him to like running, and the games teacher had been so impressed that he'd put him in the football team.

I switched on my tape recorder, and wished I'd got a CD player, like most of my friends. Mum keeps working and working, but still we never seem to have any money to spare. I wonder what *he* earns. Writers are supposed to be well paid, aren't they? Because if he's living in this house and bossing everyone around he ought to be helping Mum with the expenses, oughtn't he?

Downstairs it sounded like Mum was getting tickled. Yuk! How nauseating. I turned my music up and sat at my desk, doodling and feeling cross. Next thing, I'd pulled the drawer open and found my story. I started to read what I'd written, and as I read, the downstairs noises gradually faded away and a wave of sadness came over me. I'd been expecting it to sound stupid and boring, but instead I was gripped. When I got up to the last line I knew I had to carry on because it wasn't the end of the story. There was more to come. I reached into my school bag for my pen and as I started to write, the years disappeared until I was only four again.

The dolls are on the picnic blanket with the little tiny plastic plates covered in grass and moss and stuff, but Alice Doll wants to hide. I walk along, carrying her on my head. She likes that. So do I. It's good fun seeing how long I can keep her up there before she slides off. She says she's fed up with hiding behind trees and under the hedge and she wants a new hiding place. So we go round to the side of the house. It takes ages because it's a very long way. I find the perfect hiding place for her inside a cardboard box of newspapers, only I'm worried in case she can't breathe properly under the newspapers. I stay beside her for a little while, to make sure she's all right. Then I notice a little peephole in the side gate and put my eye to it. I can see the cars going up and down the road from here — and our red car's there too, parked outside the house.

On my way back to the other dolls I notice it's beginning to rain. It feels nice on my face, and I think the sick babies would like to have a wash with real water from the sky. It seems like magic that the sky can let water out. I hope the worms in the little rockery like it too. I feel sorry for them when the soil is dry, in case they bang their heads as they wriggle along in their earthy tunnels.

Now I'm back at the picnic blanket. I take the sick babies' clothes off and spread them out so they can have their rain bath. Then I pick up Keely Doll and Miranda and we go to find a little spot under the kitchen window, where you can press yourself against the house and not get wet at all. But something horrible is happening inside the house. I've got to drop the poor dolls so I can block my ears . . .

* * *

'Ashley . . .' I jumped. Mum had come into the room without me realising. 'Dinner's ready.'

I didn't let her see that I'd got tears in my eyes. 'I'll be down in a sec.'

9 ACTING THE PART

I was sitting at the kitchen table slaving away at my French homework, wondering how much more of this hell I could take. Things had got much worse over the last fortnight. Kieran (bless him – *not*!) had gone from three press-ups to twenty. Ben was more nauseatingly perfect than ever and Mum was turning that way too. The homework was taking me ages because I was determined not to ask *him* for any help, and Mum couldn't speak French to save her life.

I must have been sighing or looking hacked off or something, because she suddenly said,

'Why don't you just wait till Ben gets back? He won't be long, then he can help you.'

'No.'

'Suit yourself.'

'Huh! I can't suit myself any more in this house. Everything's different since *he's* been here. I'm sure I'd be much better at this stupid French if my brain had had a break.'

'Oh, not that again,' said Mum, giving me one of her 'exasperated mother' looks. 'I thought you'd accepted that it's best to get your homework out of the way as soon as you get home from school.'

'No I haven't! I think it's a stupid idea. I only do it because there's no point in arguing now *he's* God round here. Honestly, Mum, he's brainwashed you into agreeing with everything he thinks. I tell you, it's driving me mad.'

'Just give it more time. Think of Kieran – he hated Ben's influence at first, didn't he? And now look at the pair of them. They're like best mates!'

'Yuk!' I said under my breath.

Mum pounced on me. 'I think that's half the trouble, isn't it?'

'What?'

'You're jealous of Kieran.'

'Don't be stupid!' I screeched. 'Of course I'm not!'

I was expecting Mum to come back at me, but she just raised her eyebrows, then carried on making the tea, while I stared at my French textbook with a big scowl on my face. He'd even got her acting all calm and sensible like him. Anyone'd think *he* was the father and she was the new stepmother.

'Why d'you let him make decisions? What's it got to do with *him* whether I do my homework straight away after school, or leave it till later? It doesn't make any difference, does it?'

'Doesn't it?'

She was doing it again – that calm, collected thing, as though nothing I said could rattle her.

'No, it doesn't!' I snapped.

'Hmm,' she said, 'We'll see about that in a couple of weeks.'

'What do you mean?'

'There's a parents' evening coming up, isn't there?'

'Oh great! More pressure!' I sighed an exaggerated sigh then looked back at my stupid French, which made less and less sense by the minute. But a few seconds later I nearly shot into the air as I suddenly realised something. 'You're not going with Ben to the parents' evening, are you? You'd better be going with Dad –'

'Dad's perfectly happy for Ben and me to go together,' Mum answered quietly.

'Well, *I'm not!*' I slammed my hands down on the kitchen table as the back door opened.

In came Golden Boy, all red and gasping. 'Guess . . . what, Mum! I've . . . cut my time . . . by two seconds!'

Behind him was his stupid trainer, carrying the stopwatch and grinning his head off.

Mum clapped her hands together. 'You're so brilliant, Kieran!' Then she kind of slinked up to Ben and tapped him on the nose. 'And your trainer's not bad either!'

Oh, spare me! I got up, scraping my chair as loudly as I could, grabbed my books and rushed to the door. Anything to get out of their cosy little circle.

'Tea in ten minutes!' Mum called after me.

I picked up the phone from the hall table, went into the sitting room and rang Luce.

'Hi, it's me.'

'Hi, Ash. You OK?'

'No. I'm sick of this whole set-up. They're all getting on my nerves.'

Her voice went into concerned mode. 'Poor you!'

'The trouble is, I'm the only one who actually hates Ben's guts, now that Kieran's turned into his number one fan.'

'Do you actually hate him then, Ash?'

'Well . . . not exactly. He gets on my nerves though, and I just don't want him here.'

I was about to carry on but Mum came in.

She saw me on the phone and gave me a bit of a stern look because I'd broken the *always-ask-before-you-use-the-phone* rule. 'Have you seen the paper?'

I shook my head.

'Just two more minutes, Ashley, all right?'

As soon as she'd gone out I carried on bending Luce's ear about how stressed out I was. We'd moved on to discussing the French homework and I was just getting a few of the answers off her, when Mum came back in. She didn't look at all happy when she saw that I was still on the phone. 'I said two minutes and you've been nearly ten!' she hissed at me. I nodded vaguely without even looking at her, and she went out.

'Have you seen what's on tonight?' said Luce. 'The Brit Awards!'

'Yeah. I probably won't be allowed to watch it –'

'Well, you'd better insist because I'll want to talk about it in big detail tomorrow.'

I laughed just as Ben came in looking more than a bit cross. 'I thought your mother told you to get off the phone,' he said in a very tight voice.

'Uh-oh,' said Luce on the other end. 'I heard that. You'd better go. Seeya tomorrow, Ash.'

'No, it's OK,' I replied calmly, because I'd decided that this time I wasn't going to let him butt in with his clever stepfather act. I turned my back on him and carried on talking.

But I'd hardly got two words out of my mouth when the phone was whipped out of my hand and disconnected.

I leapt off the settee and started shouting. 'What d'you do that for?'

'To show you that you can't go on acting like a rude teenager.'

'I'm not acting being a teenager, I *am* one. Whereas *you're* acting like a stepfather, and that's something you'll never be!'

And with that I slammed out of the room and went upstairs two at a time.

10 MUMMY BEAR, STEPDADDY BEAR AND BABY BEAR

'Ashley, I'm talking to you. You're on another planet today!'

I sat up in my chair and tried to bring myself back to the English lesson. 'Sorry . . .'

Poor old Mercy was on about the essay he'd set us for homework, and all I could think about was running away from home, and where I'd go.

Then he said something surprising. 'That was a very good effort from you, Ashley, and there was one paragraph in particular that I was impressed with . . .'

Please don't let it be the one about the dolls' picnic . . . Or if it is, just don't say the word 'dolls'!

'The one about the picnic.'

Phew!

He was kind of beating time in the air with my essay, and eyeballing me as though he really wanted to get this message across. 'If the whole essay had had the feel of that particular paragraph, I would have given you an A. As it is you've still got a B, so well done.'

I couldn't help feeling pleased. This was the first time I'd ever got more than a C for English.

Luce whispered something. I glanced across the aisle at her. She was looking really happy for me.

Mercy was looking at me over his glasses. 'This only confirms my feeling that you've got a great deal more creative ability than you choose to demonstrate.' He looked round the whole class. 'I have the sneaky suspicion that quite a few of you might be able to muster up a bit of creativity when I tell you that I've organised a story competition . . .'

Big groans, from the boys mainly.

'. . . *and* I've managed to get a writer called Jeremy Powell to come and present the prize for the story competition . . .'

Even more groans.

'. . . which is – wait for it – twenty-five pounds!'

The groans turned to cheers.

'When's it have to be in by, Mr Mercer?' asked Max Taylor, the class comic.

Everyone laughed.

Jeremy Powell . . . I recognised that name from somewhere. Yes, that was it. There were a couple of books by someone called Jeremy Powell in Ben's office. Oh great! If Ben read books by this guy, there was no way I'd be interested in them.

At break time we were talking about my mark.

'Let's have a read then,' said Luce, trying to get the essay off me.

I handed it over. 'OK, but don't laugh.'

'Hey, that's *good*!' she said after a minute. 'I can see why Mercy likes the dolls' picnic bit best.'

I hadn't been expecting that. I felt quite pleased.

'I actually wrote a whole story about that . . . but I thought it was stupid.'

'You didn't throw it away, did you?'

I shook my head. 'It's in my desk at home, but it's not finished.'

'You ought to enter it for the competition, Ashley!'

'No, it's too . . . personal.'

'Can I see it?'

I hesitated. 'Maybe.'

When Luce and I were coming out of school at three-thirty, I spotted Ben in the distance on his way to watch Kieran play in the football match.

'Good,' I said to Luce as we got on the bus.

'At least I don't have to put up with him at home.'

Luce grinned. 'You won't be doing your homework straight away, then?'

'No chance!'

'So why don't we go into town together?'

'Yeah, cool! Only problem is I haven't got any money.'

'We'll call in at my place first. You can borrow some. I've got loads saved.'

I was just thinking that I might buy myself some nice new earrings or some make-up or something when Michelle's voice cut into my excitement. 'What time's *he* getting back then?'

I didn't bother to turn round. 'Whenever the match finishes. Five-thirty? Six?'

'You'd better make sure you're home.'

Then I *did* turn round. What did Michelle care what time I got home? 'Why?'

She looked out of the window. 'Well, you know – so he's not mad or anything.'

I didn't reply. She'd got me puzzled. I bet

Michelle never gets home on time, and yet she looked genuinely worried about me. None of us spoke till Luce's bus stop.

'See you tomorrow,' said Michelle, as Luce and I got up to go. 'Good luck with the step-pain!'

Weird!

'Get that one,' said Luce.

'I really like them both.'

'Get them both then. I don't mind. You can pay me back whenever.'

We were looking at thumb rings. The two I wanted weren't very wide but they'd got the most beautiful patterns on them.

'Trouble is, I really want that hair colour stuff as well.'

In the end I bought one of the silver rings with a black pattern, and the hair dye.

By the time we got back to Luce's it was five-thirty.

'I'd better get going. They'll be back soon.'

So I set off running, and got puffed out in no time at all. I blamed it on my heavy school bag, but really I knew it was just that I wasn't very fit. After a couple of minutes I tried again but my legs felt tight and I guessed my face was like a beetroot. I slowed down, and that's when I heard my mobile ringing.

It said *Home* on my little screen. Bummer. It was obviously *him* checking up on me. I switched it off and slowed down even more to give myself time to work out a good excuse for being late.

He was standing at the front gate looking out for me. *Great!*

'Where've you been? And why didn't you answer your phone?'

'I went to Luce's. We had this project to do . . . for English.'

'Why didn't you phone?'

'You weren't here.'

'You could have phoned my mobile.' I was near enough to see his face, all sharp and . . . clean. The sight of it made me want to tip a vacuum bag over his head. He was such a goody-goody! Why had Mum got herself hooked up with this complete wuss? 'Still, you're here now.' The sharp look kind of melted away. 'What was the project about?'

'I couldn't be bothered to explain.'

He glanced at my hands. 'Where did you get the ring from?'

'Luce.'

He didn't make any comment and we went inside.

Kieran came bursting into the kitchen, like a party hat from a cracker. 'I scored one of the goals!' he announced proudly.

'Yo! Raise the flag!'

His bright eyes turned dark. 'You're always stressy and horrible these days!'

I didn't even bother to reply, just walked out,

even though I was dying for something to eat.

From the other side of the door I could hear Ben talking to Kieran in his gentle voice. 'Your mum'll be home soon. She'll be thrilled.'

Soothe, soothe. Don't make me puke!

I got the hair colourant out of my bag and went into the bathroom.

'Omigod! What have you done?'

My heart was hammering like mad because I knew I'd gone too far. Mum was staring at my dark reddish-purple hair in big alarm.

He came up to see what the fuss was about, his faithful little shadow behind him.

'You look terrible!' said the shadow.

'Mind your own business!' I left them all with their mouths hanging open, went calmly into my room and shut the door.

'No, leave her,' I heard Mum say.

Then they all padded downstairs.

Mummy bear, stepdaddy bear and baby bear.

My bedroom mirror didn't make my hair colour look any better than the bathroom mirror did. I rushed back to the bathroom and studied the empty container. FADES AFTER SEVEN OR EIGHT WASHES. That meant that if I spent the whole evening washing it, I'd be back to normal by the time I went to bed.

As I massaged half a bottle of shampoo into my scalp I suddenly had an even better idea. Why not just leave my hair stiff with shampoo so it could work away in its own time. Cool! I draped a towel round my shoulders and went back to my room.

They were eating tea downstairs. I could hear the sound effects. My stomach was rumbling like mad but nobody was even bothering to tell me to come down. They probably preferred it without me. I pulled my story out of the desk drawer and started to read, slowly at first then faster and faster.

Then I began to write. It was like the words

were gathering round me and pulling me back to that four-year-old state again.

I'm pressed against the house to keep myself and Keely and Miranda out of the rain, but they're not out of the rain. They're lying on the ground getting soaked. My hands are tight against my ears and I'm turning my head from side to side. Mummy and Daddy are arguing. Again. Only this time it's even worse than usual. I shake my head faster and start humming loudly. It doesn't block out the angry shouty voices though, so I open my mouth to make the humming stronger. My head feels as though it's going to fall off. I've got to stop shaking it, just for a minute. I take my hands off my ears and the angry voices are too horrible to bear. Mummy is screaming. It's the worst noise I've ever heard. I've got to get away. I run round the side of the house and crouch down beside the newspaper box. That's better. I can only hear the noise of the rain in the gutter now. It's making my face and my clothes all wet but I don't mind. It's better than listening to that screaming.

Then I hear something else — a door banging. Only I can't remember which door it is. And straight after that another door bangs. I recognise this one. It's our car. I race over to look through the peephole in the gate. The windscreen wipers are tick-tocking very fast. I can see Daddy's angry face behind them. Then the car makes a screechy sound and goes zooming away. I keep my eye at the peephole, to see if it might come back again.

But it doesn't. From behind me I hear a horrible gulpy noise and when I turn round, Mummy's standing there with her face all screwed up. Her voice sounds shrill and stabby. 'What are you doing round here, Ashley? How many times have I told you to stay round the back?'

There must be something wrong with the inside of my mouth because the loudest I can talk is a whisper. 'Where's Daddy gone?'

And even though it was so soft, the moment I've said the words, I wish I could push them all back *inside my mouth because Mummy is yelling at me and I can't tell if she's talking or crying. 'He's just gone, OK? Now, get round the back. That blanket's getting soaked. I told you not to come out in the rain. You're a naughty girl!'*

My legs seem to have gone wrong just like the inside of my mouth because I can hardly keep up with Mummy. She's walking in big cross strides round to the back, and I'm wishing I'd been a good girl and done as I was told, then Daddy wouldn't have gone away in a big temper.

Then I realise my hand doesn't seem to be working either. I can hardly hold the pen, I'm shaking so much. And from just below my ribs a pain is rising higher and higher. There's nothing I can do to stop it. It's coming up into my throat and a moment later I break into sobs, and let myself fall forwards, my arms cradling my head on the desk. I can feel foamy wetness from my hair sliding on my hands and seeping through my school jumper. I push the story out of the way.

And next thing I hear Mum's voice right behind me. It's like I'm caught in some kind of weird limbo land where I don't know if I'm four or thirteen. 'It's all right, love,' she says, leaning over me, the side of her face against the back of my soapy head. She's kneeling down, her arm round my shaking shoulders. 'It's all right . . . It's all right . . .'

11 AFTER THE STORM, THE SILENCE

It's been two days since Ben went. There's no trace of him left. Well, no real trace – no computer or clothes or anything.

But there are plenty of reminders that he used to live here – Kieran's face, for a start. And if I'm up in my room and hear grunts coming from the kitchen, I know it's Kieran doing his press-ups or sit-ups or squat thrusts or something.

It happened the day after the bad hair day. Kieran and I had come home from school to find Mum at home and Ben gone. Mum had told us very calmly that she'd decided it was for the best if Ben moved out. She'd stressed that she'd still be seeing him but said that she thought perhaps, with hindsight, it had been a bit too soon for him to be actually living here. Kieran had turned a daggers look on me and said, 'Satisfied?' then marched out of the room. Mum had followed him out and I'd known she'd be giving him a little pep talk about not blaming Ashley because it wasn't really her fault, and all that stuff.

At least I didn't have to think about doing my homework or watching less telly, or not spending so much time on the phone. And I didn't have to put up with having such a goody-goody clever clogs around all the time. Better still, Mum had said we were OK on our own after school till she came home at seven. I could always phone Granny if anything went wrong. *No chance of that! I don't want Sidney Eliott to come running*. Kieran didn't talk to me much these days. It wasn't that he *wasn't* talking to me, just that we didn't have anything to say to each other.

I spent more time than ever in my room now because I was making the collage for Mum and I wanted her to really love it. I'd got it in my head that I wouldn't feel so guilty if she was pleased with her out-of-the-blue present.

Sitting on the floor with photos all around me, my eyes kept on drifting over to my desk, and that made my head fill up with thoughts about what had happened two days ago. I'd let Mum cuddle me for a few minutes, then I'd told her I wanted to be on my own again because I was scared that she might see what I'd been writing and start to try and get me to talk about it. There was no way I could do that. I couldn't even bear to *think* about it. The second she'd gone out I'd stuffed it in my school bag, thinking that I'd give it to Luce. And I'd tell her to make sure she threw it away when she'd finished.

Writing everything down seems so long ago, even though it's only two days. The worst of the red had gone out of my hair by the next morning, and it's faded a bit more since then. I quite like the way it looks now. Mum doesn't. She says I look brassy. She doesn't like my thumb ring either. Apparently you have to have long thumbs to get away with wearing rings on them. I don't care what she says – I keep it on all the time, even in school.

I've taken it off now though because it was getting in the way of my scissors as I trimmed the photos for the collage.

It was when I was cutting round a photo of Mum and me that there came an ear-piercing scream from the kitchen below.

Omigod! I went crashing downstairs to find Kieran in the kitchen, clutching his hand and looking as though he was about to faint.

'What have you done? Show me!'

He moved his top hand. It was covered in

blood. The other was even worse. 'I can't find any tissues,' he mumbled.

I rushed off to get a loo roll then came back and wrapped it around and around his hand. The blood stopped seeping through when I was on about the seventh layer. 'How did you cut it?'

He nodded at the floor by the bin. He'd been cleaning his football boots with a penknife. 'God, Kieran! What's wrong with a scrubbing brush?'

'The studs are all caked up solid and I thought I might clog up the sink if I did it with water. Ben said –'

'Yeah, OK!' I snapped, so we didn't have to suffer the entire gospel according to Saint Ben. 'Hold that tight. I'll go and get a bandage from the first aid box.' I glanced at my watch. Six-fifteen. 'Mum'll be back soon and she can decide if it needs stitches or anything.'

So I rushed off to the bathroom cabinet and found it pretty well empty. *What the* . . . Then I remembered – It was *Ben's* first aid box, wasn't it? Mum would never be that organised, even though she's a nurse.

'We haven't got a bandage, not even a bit of elastoplast,' I said, crashing back into the kitchen. Big red dots were appearing in the loo paper and Kieran's face looked very white. 'Wrap some more round. I'll go and get a bandage from Granny's.'

He nodded and I set off at a hundred miles an hour.

Even though I was gasping and aching by the time I got there, I felt quite pleased with myself because I'd been so quick. I looked at my watch and reckoned it couldn't have taken me more than three or four minutes, yet it usually took nearly ten to walk it.

Why do you care about exercise all of a sudden, Ashley? Stop being such a wuss!

I knocked on Granny's door.

'Oh dear, what's happened now?' were her first words.

'Kieran's cut his hand. It's nothing much but we haven't got a bandage or any plasters.' I was playing it down. I didn't want her thinking that the moment Ben wasn't there something had gone wrong.

Sidney was at the kitchen table, tucking into an enormous slice of fruit cake. 'Hello, young lady!' he said, spitting crumbs all over the place.

Granny told him why I was there as she reached into a jam jar for a plaster. (Granny keeps everything in jam jars.)

'I don't suppose you've got any bigger ones?' I asked.

She handed me another four, the same size. 'That's all I've got, I'm afraid. Shall I come round and have a look?'

Sidney was up like a shot, brushing cake crumbs off his trousers, ready for an outing, so I quickly assured Granny we were fine because Mum would be back any second, then I plunged back out again before she could insist. At her front gate I found myself looking at my watch. *You're doing it again, Ashley. Stop it!* But it was too late. I'd seen what time it was and I was determined to get home in a faster time than it had taken me to get here.

I set off at my fastest pace and didn't slow down once until I reached our house.

'Three minutes four seconds!' I breathed in amazement. 'That's incredible!'

And I didn't feel quite so puffed out this time either.

'You were fast!' said Kieran as I went in through the back door.

'Was I?' I tried to sound as though it was nothing special, but I had to admit I was pleased with myself.

After I'd stuck the plasters in a criss-cross pattern on Kieran's hand, the phone rang. Kieran grabbed it as I went to make some tea. I could tell straight away that it was Mum and that he must have been talking to her while I'd been out.

'Yeah, it's OK. She's put the plasters on, and there's no blood coming through or anything.'

I stopped clanking about with the mugs so I could hear better.

'Yeah, I know!' Kieran was saying. 'She only took about five minutes each way.'

'Three minutes four seconds actually!' I blurted out without thinking.

There was a pause, while Kieran smiled at the floor and listened to whatever Mum was saying on the other end.

'What time will she be back?' I asked as he put the phone down a minute later.

'Who?'

'Mum.'

'Dunno. That was Ben.'

I swung round and dropped the teabag on the floor. 'What's he phoning here for?'

'To check I'm OK. I rang him when you went

116

to Granny's. He was going to bring a bandage round if Granny didn't have any plasters.'

'It's got nothing to do with him. He should keep his nose out!' I snapped.

'He was quite impressed with your speed.'

All my crossness fizzled away. 'Was he?' I asked a bit pathetically.

Kieran didn't say any more, and I knew it was stupid but I wanted to know exactly what Ben had said. I tried to sound ultra-casual 'What did he say?'

Kieran turned, grinning. 'You've gone red.'

'I've been running, dur!'

'He said he knew you'd make a good runner because you've got the right legs for it.'

'What a cheek! How dare he say stuff about my legs!'

Kieran wasn't even listening. He must have become immune to my moans about Ben.

'Your tea's on the side. I'm just going to do a bit more to Mum's collage.'

But I wasn't. I was going up to check out my legs in the mirror.

12 MICHELLE'S STORY

At the end of biology Luce and I walked back to the classroom together.

'I'm such rubbish at biology, Luce. What a pathetic mark for that homework.'

She linked her arm through mine. 'You're not rubbish, Ash! Think about that brilliant mark you got for the circulation of the blood that time!'

'That was just a fluke.'

'Sure it wasn't because you had Ben around?'

I didn't answer. There was nothing I could say. She was right.

Suddenly she stopped and closed her eyes for a second. Her face was really pale. 'I feel terrible, Ash,' she whispered.

'Why?'

'Dunno.'

'Are you going to be OK?'

'No, I'm going to be sick.'

She belted off to the loos and I followed her slowly. When she came out she looked paler than ever.

'I'll take you to the nurse, Luce. You ought to go home.'

She nodded.

It was wet break. I went into the classroom. Everyone was in little clusters. The noise level was amazingly high and I wondered how long it would be until one of the teachers came in to tell us all to pipe down. Only Michelle was on her own – her nose buried in something that looked like an essay. As I went past her chair I got a shock. She was reading *my* story. How dare she!

I wanted to snatch it out of her hand, but you didn't do things like that to Michelle. 'Where did you get that?' I asked coldly.

'It's brilliant, Ashley.' Her words took the wind right out of my sails. I was expecting her to start mocking it. I leaned over to check we were talking about the same story. 'Is it . . . you know . . . true?'

I nodded.

'It's incredible!'

She was silent for a few more seconds. Feeling surprised and confused and pleased all at the same time, I watched her finish it off, then I saw she had tears in her eyes. I looked round. People were shouting and laughing and chucking things, and no one was paying any attention to Michelle and me, wrapped up in our own private little world. It was a weird moment.

'You ought to enter this for that competition that Mercy was on about.'

'No, I'd feel stupid. People'll do far better stories than this.'

'They won't, honest.' She got up and grabbed my wrist. 'Come on.'

'No, Michelle, no. I don't want to enter it.'

'Well, you've got no choice.' She dragged me down the corridor. It seemed so quiet compared to our classroom.

I protested all the way to the staffroom, even when Michelle knocked on the door and asked to speak to Mr Mercer.

'Ashley's entering this for that story competition,' she said, handing over the rather tatty-looking sheets to a very surprised-looking Mr Mercer.

He broke into a big beam. 'Super! I was hoping for a few more entries. Spread it around your friends, eh? See if you can drum up a bit more interest.'

I just stared.

As we walked back to the classroom I

noticed that Michelle was slowing her pace right down, and finally she stopped altogether. 'Ashley?' she said slowly. 'I'm entering a kind of competition too . . .'

I looked at her. She was biting her lip. I'd never seen her unsure of herself like this. 'Yeah?'

'It's a skateboarding competition called the Griggsmere.'

'Yeah?'

'Only I don't know if I'm good enough. My brother says I'm not, but then he would say that, wouldn't he?'

I wasn't sure what she was leading to.

'So I was wondering if you'd come and kind of watch me and tell me what you think.'

I felt a bit nervous but quite honoured that I'd been invited into Michelle's world. 'When?'

'After school?'

Kieran was playing in an away match after school. I knew Ben was going to watch and then Mum would be joining them at the end. I'd thought about going into town with Luce but I couldn't do that now she was ill. I'd just be going home to an empty house.

I looked at Michelle. She was fixing me with a big-eyed, hopeful look.

'Yeah, OK.'

'Cool!'

We sat at the very back of the bus, Michelle and I. We were going to get off near the multi-storey car park, then go up to the top level. I was starting to feel really nervous and wondering if I'd been stupid to agree to come. Michelle's brother and his mates were sitting at the front of the bus.

'Will your brother and the others be there?'

'Nah. He uses the ramps, or otherwise that bit by the station car park. There are steps there. Where's *your* brother?'

'Playing football. Away match.'

'So *he's* not watching then?'

I knew who she meant. 'Well, actually . . .'

She was scowling. I didn't know why. 'I thought your mum had kicked him out.'

'Yeah, she did. But Kieran still likes him – and so does Mum. It's only really me . . .'

'They're all scum, aren't they, stepfathers?'

'I dunno . . .'

'Well, yours was, and Kevin was.' She looked down and started pressing her thumbnail into the ball of her other thumb. 'I hated him. Still do.' So she *did* have a stepfather at one time. She looked at me. 'Do you still hate yours?'

I didn't really know the answer to that one. I didn't like him, I didn't want him around . . . But *hate*?

'Did he . . . you know . . . hurt you or anything?'

My heart started pounding. Michelle must have had a totally terrible time with her stepfather. I felt suddenly pathetic. The worst thing Ben had done was to butt into my life with his endless questions. I shook my head.

'You're lucky.'

I waited.

'Kevin used to . . . hurt me . . .'

My mouth felt dry. 'Poor you,' I managed to whisper.

'He didn't at first, when he was all lovey-dovey with Mum. It was later. He used to get drunk in the pub, and come back and act all . . . violent. It was ages ago . . .'

'Ages?'

'About a year.'

Everything suddenly clicked into place. I understood why Michelle had taken such an interest in how I was getting on with Ben. In her own way she was trying to look out for me – help me in the 'step-pain' war.

I wasn't sure I wanted to know the answer to my next question. 'What did you do when he came back drunk?'

'Usually I just went up to my room and put my headphones on and turned my music up.

But one time it really got to me and I kind of snapped and told him where to go. You should have seen him – he looked like he was going to boil right over. My mum screamed at me to get out of his way so I ran out of the house and down the road, but I couldn't see very well 'cos it was getting dark.'

'Where were you going?'

'To find my brother Darren. I thought he might be at his friend's, but he wasn't, so then I didn't know where to go. I didn't think it'd be safe to go back home until later . . .'

'Later?'

'Yeah. I knew he would have crashed out, same as always . . . So I was just wandering round in the dark . . .'

'It must have been awful!'

'The worst bit came next. I suddenly saw a torch blobbing around ahead of me, so I pressed myself into this hedge and my jumper got caught on the brambles. I was trying to yank it off but it was completely stuck, and that was when he made a grab for me.'

'You mean he'd come after you!'

She nodded. 'He grabbed my wrist and said I was coming home with him and no arguments because it was dangerous out there. I tried to shake him off because he still stank of drink and he was kind of swaying about. I told him no way was I coming home and that made him wild again and he yanked at my arm till I thought it was going to come out of its socket, and I yelled at him to get off me . . .'

'Omigod, Michelle! What happened?'

'Well, this bloke must have heard me shouting, because he suddenly comes running up to us out of the darkness, yelling, "Get off her! Get off her!" And just for a second Kevin loosens his grip because he's concentrating on shining the torch in the bloke's face, so I wrench myself away from him and run back home fast as anything.'

'What about the bloke?'

'Dunno. Didn't hang about long enough to find out. I heard him trying to tell Kevin to calm down as I ran off, but there was no way Kevin would calm down in that state. No way.'

'Did he come home later?'

'He tried, but Mum had got my uncle to come round by then, and everyone's scared of him because he's so big. He told Kevin to get lost and never to come back, and the next day Mum had the locks changed.'

I was thinking back to that time about a year ago when Michelle had come into the classroom with cuts and bruises and Mrs Wells had been so worried.

It all made sense now. 'Have you seen him since?'

'Nah. I think he left town. He's just not around any more. Thank God.'

13 CHURNING THINGS OVER

I watched Michelle on her skateboard for half an hour. She was incredible.

'I'd no idea you could do all that,' I told her. 'Your brother *can't* be better than you – it's impossible.'

'He's more daring than me. He takes more risks.' She grinned. 'But he comes off more often too.'

'When's the competition?'

'Tomorrow. It's more than a competition, actually. It's a whole day at this disused airfield at Griggsmere.'

'You mean you're allowed to go off during school time? Sounds wicked!'

'Well, only if you've been – you know –'

'What, selected?'

She looked down.

'Michelle, that's brilliant. You're so clever!'

She ignored that. 'They've got massive ramps and slopes and things there, and you get a certificate at the end as long as you join in with at least one of the sessions. The guys running the sessions are only about seventeen, eighteen. Darren says he wants to run one next year. Darren's always saying I'm rubbish, but Mum put my name forward for the trial . . .'

'So Darren got it wrong!'

'Do you think so?'

'I *know* so.'

She grinned.

I ran all the way home – well, nearly all the way. I walked the last fifty metres because I didn't want any lip from Kieran about me looking puffed out. As it happened, they didn't get back for another five minutes.

'Didn't you win?' I asked, seeing Kieran's glum-looking face.

'Five, two,' he snapped, 'to us.'

So what was rattling him then? I looked at Mum for clues. She shook her head to tell me to leave it, so I waited till Kieran went out.

'He's a bit fed up because he wanted Ben to come back with us, but Ben said he wouldn't.'

A massive rush of guilt hit me.

'I'm going out with him a bit later – just for a quick drink. You'll be OK on your own, will you?'

I nodded. 'Fine.'

It wasn't till tea was on the table about fifteen minutes later that I realised I'd just been in my own little world all that time, thinking how amazing it was that Michelle and I had so little, and yet so much, in common. I knew all about her mum and her stepdad's massive row, and her stepdad being kicked out. She knew all about *my* mum and dad's massive row, and my dad walking out. *She* was entering the skateboarding competition, *I* was entering the story-writing competition, and neither of us thought we were good enough, but we'd each been persuaded by the other one that we were!

'D'you fancy going to Dad's this weekend, love?' Mum's voice interrupted my thoughts.

No, I don't. I've suddenly got bad feelings about Dad.

'I don't really want to go, Mum.'

She looked at me sharply. 'But it's all arranged. I'm seeing Ben . . .'

'See him then. I don't mind. I'll go out. I just don't want to go to Dad's.'

'Why not? You usually like going.'

The question was too big. I didn't know how to answer it. 'I can't explain.'

She frowned, then went to the door and called out to Kieran that tea was ready.

The two of them chatted about the match during tea, while I went back to the world inside my head. I was thinking about those newspapers in the box outside. For as long as I can remember Mum's put old newspapers and magazines and things in a box outside. When the box is full she takes them to be recycled. But there hasn't always been a recycling centre in town.

'Mum?'

She looked up. I caught a little glimpse of hope in her face. She must have thought I was going to say that I *would* go to Dad's at the weekend, after all. She was going to be disappointed. I felt bad.

'What happened to the newspapers that you put out, before the recycling place opened?'

She looked surprised. No wonder. It must have seemed like a really weird question coming out of the blue.

'The dustman used to take them. Why?'

'Nothing . . .' *Poor Alice Doll.*

Something sad must have shown on my face. Mum looked so worried all of a sudden.

Maybe I could give her a little bit more. 'I was just thinking back to when I was little. I . . . hid something in the newspaper box, that's all. I was only wondering what might have happened to it.'

'What d'you hide?' asked Kieran with his mouth full.

'Just . . . a toy . . .'

He carried on chewing, but I could tell I'd got him thinking. He turned to Mum. 'Ben's researching something about toys, isn't he?'

Mum nodded and smiled. She was all shiny-eyed at the mention of *his* name.

Kieran went on talking with his mouth full. 'I don't get why he has to go to the library. Why can't he get stuff off the Internet?'

'I think it's quite a nice break from the

computer. He says he's no good at writing after four o'clock, so he might as well go out and meet a few real people.'

After tea I went up to my room and lay on my bed. I kept on going over and over what had happened to Michelle. It churned up my insides and made me wish I had a massive great vacuum cleaner to hoover all the bad stuff out of the world. Nowhere felt safe. I knew it was pathetic and babyish but I couldn't stop thinking about my dolls. You're lucky when you're only four, because you can cuddle dolls and toys and things. Miranda Doll would have been perfect to cuddle at this moment – all soft and big . . .

Oh stop being such a wuss, Ashley! I jumped off the bed and went over to my desk. *Miranda Doll isn't the only big, soft thing round here!* Right. Homework.

I opened my book and made myself

concentrate. I was going to prove to Mr Jones that the circulation of the blood test hadn't just been a flash in the pan.

14 DEFENDING THE INNOCENT

Luce wasn't back at school the next day, and of course Michelle was away at the Griggsmere competition. I kept on wondering how she was doing. Maybe I'd give her a ring in the evening. It was odd without either of them at school. Even the school itself looked odd because there were posters advertising Jeremy Powell's latest book, *Defending the Innocent*, everywhere you looked. Mercy says that Jeremy Powell writes novels for adults usually, but this one's for teenagers, so that's why he's coming to our school.

I've been sitting on my own in most of the lessons and found myself getting down to work really well. All the teachers have been gobsmacked, and I know Ben would have been proud of me.

Ben? Proud? What was I thinking? Why should I care about that? I shook my head to make the stupid thought go away.

After school I sat on the bus and stared out of the window. Kieran had gone to a friend's house for tea. Mum wouldn't be back till seven. I wished she was going to be home early for once, then I could tell her how the geography teacher had asked me to stay back at the end of the lesson to tell me that she really thought I could do well if I kept my new attitude up.

Maybe I'd go round and tell Granny.

On the other hand, maybe not. *He'd* be there, wouldn't he? Sidney the cake-spitter.

I decided to go into town and walk round

the shops. I didn't have any money but who cared? I could try a few things on . . .

So I got off the bus and headed for the precinct. But when I got there I went straight past. I knew, really, that I'd never had any intention of going to the shops. I was going to the library. That's where Ben would be. Kieran had said so, hadn't he? My heart was hammering away because I didn't know what I was going to say when I got there, and of course I couldn't be absolutely certain that he *would* be there. All I knew was that I wanted to tell him about the geography teacher – and perhaps mention that Michelle had read my dolls' picnic story and she'd thought it was good enough to enter the competition. And I could tell him that my running speed was even better than that time from Granny's and maybe he'd be interested to hear about Michelle and the Griggsmere competition. And then there was the circulation of the blood test. . . . Oh yes, and Jeremy Powell, that author – I wondered if Ben knew he'd written a book for teenagers.

My pace quickened. But the clock on the Town Hall said just after four o'clock. He might not even be there yet . . .

I pushed open the big swing door and headed for the reference section. It was round the corner of the L shape.

And then I saw him – talking to someone. He had his back to me. *She* didn't, but *she* didn't notice me. She was too busy flirting with him, in her short skirt and tight top. It made me sick the way she was looking up at him with her smiley eyes and pouty pink lips. Whatever he was saying to her must have been incredibly witty because she suddenly broke into loud, tinkly laughter. I felt like throwing up. Ben was seeing someone else. How dare he do this to Mum!

* * *

'How did it go, Michelle?' I called out, the moment I saw her coming in the classroom the next day.

She looked a bit embarrassed. 'I was runner-up in the under-fifteens.'

'Hey, fantastic!'

'That's brilliant!' said Luce. 'Ashley told me about the competition last night.'

'What did Darren say?' I asked Michelle.

She grinned. 'He only managed third place in the under-eighteens, so he was well impressed with me!'

Mrs Wells came in at that moment. 'Come and tell me all about your day, Michelle. I was crossing my fingers for you!'

So Luce and I went back to our own conversation about Ben and the library and what had happened since we'd had our phone chat.

'Honestly, Luce, I felt such a fool for thinking that he was having an affair with that woman. It turns out that she's one of the librarians.'

'How do you know?' Luce leaned forwards, eyes gleaming. 'Did you mention it to your mum?'

'No, I heard her talking on the phone to Ben. She was joking about how it must be quite boring working in a library. She said the librarian must love it when attractive men go in there! And Ben being a writer as well . . .'

Luce clapped her hand to her mouth. 'Whoops!' Then her laughing eyes turned to puzzled ones. 'I don't get why you went down to the library in the first place. I thought you hated Ben's guts.'

'I've never actually hated him – I was just so sick of all his interfering and everything.'

She spoke very quietly. 'And now he's gone, you miss the rules, right?'

I shrugged. 'Dunno.'

And that much was true. I really didn't know. It was all so confusing.

* * *

When the bell for afternoon school went, we all filed into the hall. The whole place was buzzing with the name Jeremy Powell, and everyone who'd entered the competition was hoping like mad that they might be picking up the twenty-five pounds. Well, everyone except me. The more I thought about my story, the more I realised it was stupid to have let Michelle talk me into entering it. It was so babyish.

We sat down on the floor. I was sitting between Michelle and Luce.

'Is Jeremy what's-his-name doing a talk or just presenting the prizes?' asked Michelle, looking bored before the man had even appeared.

'Mercy said it was a question-and-answer session, then the presentation of the prize.'

Luce was just folding her arms and telling us she wouldn't have a clue what kind of questions to ask a writer, when Mr Mercer came into the hall through the back door. Immediately the noise level went down and everyone turned round to see what the great writer looked like.

'Omigod!' said Luce, nudging me violently in the ribs. 'Have you seen who it is!'

I gasped. There, in his smartest clothes, striding up the aisle after Mercy, was Ben. My mouth dropped open, then I quickly shut it and stared at a black mark on the floor. I didn't think I'd be able to look up till it was all over and he'd gone. It would be awful if our eyes met.

'Jeremy Powell must be ill or something,' Luce hissed, 'so they had to ask Ben.'

On the other side of me Michelle gasped too. 'You mean that's your –?'

'Yeah,' I said before she could say the dreaded word.

Then there was complete silence and Mercy began his introduction. 'I'm absolutely delighted to be able to welcome Mr Jeremy Powell to our school this afternoon. He is the author of a number of adult novels, and as you all know, his latest novel, *Defending the Innocent* is for teenagers . . .'

'Why's he calling him Jeremy Powell?' asked Luce a bit too loudly.

Her voice rang out and made Mercy look over in our direction. 'Aha!' he said, looking pleased with the way things were going. 'Good question, Luce. Let's ask Jeremy himself to answer that one!'

I kept my eyes on the floor but I could feel my cheeks going red because I knew Ben would be looking in our direction.

'Jeremy Powell is my pen name,' he said clearly and calmly. 'My real name is Ben Willis. Some authors prefer to write under a pen name to keep their private life separate from their working life.'

'Do writers earn loads of money?' called out a loud year-nine boy.

I risked looking up then, because the boy was sitting right at the other side of the hall from me.

'Depends how popular their books are,' Ben replied. Then he suddenly grinned and made a big thing of examining his jacket. 'If they're not particularly popular, then they have to make do with just the one suit for all occasions!'

Everyone burst into laughter, and I felt quite proud that Ben was proving to be a hit at my school.

Proud? What was I thinking? Why should I be proud? He's nothing to do with me.

Luce nudged me again. 'He's good, isn't he?'

I didn't say anything but I couldn't resist glancing at Michelle to see what she made of him. When I saw her white face and staring eyes I got a shock. 'Are you OK, Michelle? What's the matter?'

She gulped and stared straight ahead of her

as though she'd seen a ghost. Then, in no more than a whisper, she said, 'Tell you after.'

A girl in the front row had her hand up. Mercy nodded to tell her to go ahead and ask her question.

'Are you writing a book at the moment,' she began hesitantly.

'I've just finished one, actually.'

'Wh – when's it going to be published?'

'Ah!' said Ben. 'I'm afraid the answer is that I don't know. I sent it off to the publisher a little while ago and I'm waiting to hear whether or not they like it. I'm hoping they will because it's very special to me.'

'Is it for teenagers or adults?'

'Teenagers.'

I found it hard to concentrate after that, because Michelle seemed to be in such a state and I couldn't imagine what was the matter with her. Question after question was fired at Ben and he answered them all in quite a witty way, which went down very well with the boys especially.

Then after about twenty minutes Mr Mercer said, 'Right, let's move on to the part of Jeremy's visit that I know you've all been looking forward to.' He smiled round the hall and rubbed his hands together, as though Ben was about to walk a tightrope five metres off the ground. 'Over to you, Jeremy.'

Ben reached into his tatty old briefcase and pulled out a bundle of papers. His eyes roamed round the room, so I quickly looked down again. 'I must say', he began, 'that the standard of story-writing in this school is very high indeed, and that judging this competition has been one of the hardest things I've ever had to do. After a great deal of tearing my hair out,' he pointed to his head, '– it was a lot thicker than this two weeks ago! – I've managed to pick a runner-up and a winner, and Mr Mercer has kindly allocated prize money of fifteen pounds for the runner-up.'

Everyone burst into applause at that announcement, then the whole hall held its breath. 'I'm not going to go on about why I've chosen the two particular stories that I've chosen – I'll just simply say that they moved me the most. I'm going to announce the runner-up first, and that is . . . Ashley Ross!'

My stomach turned upside-down about three times, then inside-out. 'It's you, Ashley,' hissed Luce. 'Go on – Mercy's beckoning you to go out to the front.'

'I . . . I can't . . .'

'Go on,' said Michelle, very softly. 'You deserve it. I knew I was right about your story.'

Michelle had been so still and silent ever since Ben had walked into this hall, and now she'd actually uttered a few words, I thought I ought to do as she said. It was like she was a package with the words FRAGILE, HANDLE

WITH CARE on it. I threaded my way along the row, and went out to the front on shaky jelly legs. Everyone was clapping away and I realised that hardly a single person in the hall knew that Ben was my really my step –

No, he wasn't, was he?

It was like being stuck in the middle of one of those dreams where everything's weird and wrong. He smiled at me as he shook my hand and gave me an envelope with my name on the front. I don't know if I smiled back or not. All I remember is saying thank you in a very small voice then going back to my place, heart beating, mouth dry and a strange feeling in the pit of my stomach.

Luce's eyes were shining like mad. She grabbed the envelope from me. 'Let's have a look!'

Michelle was still as pale as paper, and when I asked her if she was OK, she said she wanted to get out of the hall. I thought she might need some help, so as everyone cheered the winner of the competition from year nine, I whispered to Luce that I was just taking Michelle out because she wasn't feeling well.

We went into an empty classroom and sat down together. I stayed quiet and waited for her to tell me what had upset her.

After a few seconds she spoke in hardly more than a whisper. 'I was wrong about your stepfather. He's not like . . . my stepfather. He's a good man.'

'H – how do you know Ben?'

'Because I've seen him before. He was the man who came to help me that time when my stepdad was drunk and he came after me . . .'

Now *I* was the one to turn pale. My mouth went completely dry. I could hardly swallow. 'It was . . . Ben? Are – are you sure?'

She nodded. 'I recognised him straight away, just from seeing him that once in Kevin's torchlight. I'll never ever forget what he did for me. I know he must have got beaten up. He risked his life for me.'

My eye fell on the poster on the wall behind Michelle.

Defending the Innocent.

I gasped.

15 GETTING RID OF THE REAL PAIN

I left Michelle and went back to the hall, but I didn't dare go in. It was too quiet. People might have turned round and stared when they heard the door open. Mercy was on his feet giving a thank-you speech. After a few minutes everyone burst into loud applause, then the students at the back started filing out.

'Well done, Ashley!'

'Nice one, Ash!'

'Lucky thing, Ashley!'

I didn't want people to think I was deliberately standing there to get loads of congratulations, so I went back to my classroom and started thinking about how Mum had first met Ben. He'd been one of her patients in hospital. That was all I knew.

Luce and the others came back to the classroom and I said I was just going to the loo, because I couldn't explain why I wanted to see Ben (not even to myself).

He was talking to Mercy when I got to the hall, and a couple of year-nine girls were waiting for him to give them his autograph. They came out talking excitedly to each other about how happy their mums were going to be with the autographs. Neither of them noticed me. I was about to go in, but the head teacher suddenly appeared and beat me to it.

'Well, you certainly seem to have been a big hit,' he gushed, as he strode down the aisle towards Ben.

Then a whole group of girls followed him in, clutching their pens and papers, so I turned and headed back to the classroom. There was no point in trying to get him on his own.

Later, on the bus, I looked at the fifteen pounds. There was nothing else in the envelope. I said 'bye to Luce and wandered home. Kieran jogged ahead of me, but I didn't feel like running.

'Hello, you clever girl!' came Mum's voice as I went round the back. She was standing at the door.

It was a lovely surprise. 'What are you doing back so early?'

'Well, a little bird told me you might have some very good news today, so I thought you'd want to share it!' She gave me a big hug. 'Well done, love. Ben said your story was absolutely fantastic.'

When she said that, I suddenly realised something. 'He *had* to chose me, didn't he? I bet there were tonnes of other stories that he liked better.'

I was at the kitchen table and Mum came and sat down beside me. Kieran must have gone up to his room.

'Well, you're wrong about that, love, because he told me that he actually wanted to give you the *first* prize. He said it was the best story by a mile, but he didn't feel that he could do that, because if anyone knew that he was going out with your mum, they'd say it was unfair.'

I stared at the table and thought about that one.

Mum spoke very quietly. 'He told me what the story was about too, love.'

I didn't reply.

She reached for my hand and held it. 'It wasn't your fault, you know, Ashley.'

'What?'

'That your dad went and left us. It was nothing to do with you.'

I felt my throat tightening up. 'But you were so cross with me . . .'

'No, I wasn't, love. I was angry and upset with Dad and with myself, but not with you.'

'But the blanket . . .?'

'That was nothing. It just got caught up in the whole situation.'

'I thought it was me.'

Mum hugged me tight and I could feel tears on my face again, only this time they weren't mine. 'Oh Ashley, I can't bear to think of what you've been going through. I promise nothing was your fault.' Her voice went faint. 'You were just a little girl having a dolls' picnic in the rain.'

And then it was me trying to make Mum feel better. 'It's OK, Mum. I'm not upset any more. Now I understand.'

Her voice was still faint. 'Ben felt so sorry for you. When he read your story he realised how much you were hurting inside.'

I nodded and we were both silent for a while. But there was one more thing I wanted to talk about. 'Alice got taken away by the dustman, didn't she?'

Mum nodded and wiped her tears away with her hand. She smiled at me. 'But not all the dolls liked hiding, did they? So when you asked about the newspapers I got thinking, and I decided to have a rummage through all the stuff in the attic. Go and have a look in your room.'

We ran upstairs together and I pushed open my bedroom door slowly. There, on my bed, in an old torn dress, was Miranda Doll. I felt tears coming into my eyes as I went to pick her up and clutched her tight. 'That's so brilliant, Mum! I thought we'd chucked out all my old things. And look,' I put Miranda Doll down and reached under my bed for the collage, 'this is for you.'

'Oh Ashley, it's lovely! I mean . . . what a present!'

We went straight to hang it up on the nail where the clip frame had been before, then we stood on the stairs and studied it for a bit, reminding each other of the exact moment when all the photos had been taken. Kieran came along and joined in, helping us out with some of the ones of him.

After he'd gone back in his room. Mum and I went down to the kitchen. There was something I wanted to ask her – something I'd been thinking about ever since Michelle had told me that she recognised Ben.

'You know when you first met Ben, when he was a patient in hospital?'

'Yes.'

'Well, what was he in hospital for?'

'He had a broken rib and a few other more minor injuries.'

'Do you know how he got the injuries?'

'Yes, I do.' She looked at me carefully. 'Do you?'

I nodded. 'My friend Michelle recognised him. She said she'd never forget how he helped her.'

Mum nodded slowly. 'He's a good man.'

'That's what Michelle said. And I was going to tell him, after his talk, but there were so many people around all the time.'

'You could tell him now if you want.'

'What? Phone him?'

'I phoned him earlier on to tell him a letter came for him in the post. He's calling round to collect it. But he won't be staying,' she added quickly.

'What time is he coming?'

'He said he was going to jog over at about five, because his car's broken down.'

I glanced at my watch. Five past five. 'I'll meet him, I think.' I realised I didn't have a clue where he lived now. 'Which way will he be coming from?'

'Graham Road way.' I made for the back door, but Mum stopped me. 'Here,' she said, handing me the letter addressed to Ben. 'Take this with you.'

* * *

I came across him after about five minutes.

'Hi,' he called. 'I was just coming round to your place to pick up a letter. I'm hoping it might be from my publisher.'

I handed it to him. 'I've got it here. It looks kind of official.'

He ripped it open and scanned it quickly, then punched his fist in the air and said, 'Yesssss!'

'So it *is* the publishers!' I said excitedly.

'Certainly is!' He looked as though he couldn't stop grinning. 'And they've accepted my book!'

'Hey, cool, Ben! You're so clever!' I grabbed his arm. 'Quick, let's go and tell Mum.'

So we set off, jogging side by side. 'That story, Ashley – it was one of the best things I've read for a long time.'

'Mum said you liked it,' I puffed. 'And guess what? She found Miranda Doll in the attic!'

'Excellent!'

'And I've given her the collage.'

'And what did she reckon?'

'She loved it! And . . .'

But we were home by then and Mum was at the door, smiling at us. 'Well?'

'Great news! They've bought it!'

'Oh Ben, that's wonderful!' She rushed out and gave him a big hug, then took his hand to bring him into the house.

He seemed to be hanging back though.

'Hiya, Ben!' called Kieran, leaning out of his bedroom window. 'Are you staying for a while?'

Ben turned to me. He didn't actually speak, but his eyes were saying, *What do you think, Ashley?*

'I've got loads of stuff to tell you,' I said.

But still he didn't go in.

'Come on!' said Mum. 'You can stay a little while . . . surely?'

Again he looked at me.

'Yeah, stay,' I said quietly.

He smiled then. And we went into the house together.

What happens next in the step-chain?
Meet Joe in . . .

Step-Chain

SHE WANTS WAR?

1 SUFFERING THE WISECRACKS

'So what d'you watch last night?'

That's Jack, and he's looking at me. I'm feeling quite smug because Dad and I have got satellite TV. It's just about the only luxury we *have* got, but still . . . 'The match on Sky,' I tell him, grinning.

'Yeah, OK, you don't have to rub it in,' says Andy.

Dean's writing away like a maniac, trying to get his French homework done before the bell goes. He always leaves everything till the last minute, Dean does. He still manages to talk though. 'Did you see *The Grotes*?'

Oh great! I'd forgotten that stupid programme was on last night.

'Wicked, wasn't it?' says Andy, leaning forward. 'What about that bit when Mac left those sweets lying around where he knew his sister would nick a few?'

Dean stops writing and looks up. 'Yeah, the look on her face when she tastes them!'

'Imagine being Mac Grote, and having to put up with a twin sister. It'd be gross, wouldn't it?' says Jack, pulling a face, then giving me an over-the-top grin from point blank range.

Now I'm in for a load of mickey-taking. I wouldn't care if it was about something else – anything but *this*.

I try and get them back. 'Ha ha! Very funny. Don't you get fed up with cracking the same jokes all the time?' I know I'm on to a loser.

Dean's got this clever look on his face. 'Just think,' he says, 'once your dad's moved in with

Eleanor's mum, us lot won't *have* to watch *The Grotes* on Sunday nights. We'll just come round to your place and watch you and Eleanor.'

The others fall about. I ought to ignore them and wait till they get bored with the subject, but it's not easy when you're mad.

Ever since Dad broke the news to me that he and his girlfriend were planning on moving in together, I've had to put up with these wisecracks. I wish I'd never told my mates. I don't know how much longer I can put up with it. It's bad enough having to move in with a bunch of girls, especially when one of them's the same age as you, but it makes it ten times worse when your mates think it's one big laugh. It's not that I don't like Eleanor Stern – I do. And if she'd always been my stepsister I'd be fine with it. But she hasn't. So now it seems like a big deal – this 'moving in together' thing. I tell you it makes you feel a right ponce.

'You're only jealous!' I say.

'Oh yeah, like I'd rather live with Eleanor Stern and her fat-cheeked sister than live with two brothers!' That's Jack.

'Well, I'd swap Eleanor Stern with my sister any day,' says Andy.

We all crack up because it's no secret that Andy fancies Eleanor like mad, and his big sister drives him nutty.

He goes red and turns on Dean. 'I don't know what *you're* laughing at!' You've got a sister the same age as Eleanor *Stern's* sister!'

So then Dean looks a bit embarrassed too, and I'm feeling quite pleased with the way I'm getting off the hook here. Until . . .

'Wooo! Look who it is!' That's Jack.

My heart sinks. Kelly Grey, from the same class as Eleanor, is standing in our classroom doorway, grinning all over her stupid face.

'She so fancies you, Joe!' Andy whispers into the back of my neck.

'Well, I don't fancy *her*! I snap back,

pretending to look for something in my school bag.

'She's coming over!' says Dean, grinning. 'This is going to be good.'

My whole body groans. Kelly Grey wears tonnes of black stuff on her eyes and it's obvious she dyes her hair because you can see two different colours. She's got a stud in her tongue too.

'Hiya. What are you lot talking about then?'

'Joe and Eleanor moving in together,' says Jack.

'Not us. Our parents,' I snap.

Kelly comes and puts her arm round me. Gross. 'Leave him alone,' she says in this really drippy voice. 'You've upset him now.'

I can feel her left boob pressing against my arm and it's making my face hot. 'Get off, Kelly. I'm OK.'

'You've gone red, Joe,' says Andy.

He can talk.

She moves her arm, thank God, but she's still determined to embarrass me. 'Don't listen to them, Joe. It'll be nice at Eleanor's. And you'll have a brand new mum, won't you?'

I feel like someone's rammed a knife into my stomach. 'I'm going to the toilet.'

Nobody says a word as I go striding off, but when I'm halfway to the door I hear Dean hissing at Kelly, 'What d'you have to say that for?'

Then she starts protesting like mad. 'What? I'm only saying what Eleanor said. What's wrong with that?'

I don't go the toilet – just walk round for a bit, thinking. How dare Eleanor Stern say that! I thought she was quite nice . . . until now. I don't want a new mum. I never will. It's more than two years since my mum died but I still get this stabbing thing sometimes, and that's what's just happened, only worse than usual.

If Eleanor Stern thinks *her* mum's going to take the place of mine, she can bug off. It's bad enough just *thinking* that. But going round telling people – that's gross.

I just wish Kelly stupid Grey had never come into our classroom. She's ruined everything now. Eleanor's mum is Dad's girlfriend. She's OK. I like her. But she's just Sylvia to me, and that's all she'll ever be.

At home later, I'm eating egg and chips with Dad and letting him know he's ruining my life.

'You don't know what it's like, Dad. Dean and the others take the mick the whole time about me and Eleanor living together. Why can't you and Sylvia just keep going out with each other?'

'What? You mean till *you* say it's OK for us to move in?'

He's twisting it to make it sound like I'm the selfish one. Right . . . 'She's got this stupid friend called Kelly Grey . . .'

'Who has?'

'Eleanor. Who d'you think? And she fancies me . . .'

'Who does?'

He can be so thick sometimes. 'Keep up, Dad. Kelly Grey!'

'Lucky *you*!'

'Shut up! She's hideous.'

He grins. *Can* someone *take me seriously, please*?

'I know what's going to happen, Dad. The moment we move in, she'll be round at Eleanor's, getting in my face. It's going to be so embarrassing. Why can't that lot just move here? That wouldn't be half so bad. I'd be more – you know – in control, then.'

'Oh come on, Joe, we've been through this hundreds of times. Sylvia's house is bigger than ours and it's nearer to school and everything. What's the point in her uprooting four of them when there are only two of us to move?'

I feel like telling him what Eleanor's been

going round saying. That'd make him think again. But I don't, because I don't want to bring Mum into this. I can't take that stabbing thing again. No thanks.

'Look, why don't you just come round to Sylvia's?'

'Not that again, Dad.'

'But why won't you? Don't you want to see what your new home's going to be like?'

'No.' How can I explain that it'd make me feel stupid – like a little kid? No, like a visitor. No, more like a refugee. Because it's *their* house. 'They'll show off about it . . . and everything.'

'Eleanor's not like that. You said yourself that she's one of the nicest in year eight.'

Yeah, until today.

'And Louise wouldn't know *how* to show off, she's so shy.'

'And ugly,' I mumble under my breath. I know it's cruel the moment I've said it, but I'm mad, OK?

Unfortunately he hears. 'Don't get like that, Joe. I'm not having it. None of us can help our looks.'

I stay quiet.

'Think what it must be like for Louise, having two good-looking sisters and being . . . stuck in the middle.'

'See! You admit it! She's ugly.'

So then he changes the conversation. 'And what about Jade? You haven't even met her.'

'I've told you, I don't want to. She sounds completely off her trolley.'

'She *is* off her trolley. But I swear you'll like her. She's so . . . up front.'

The kid is six and she's up front? What's she going to be like when she's thirteen? What a terrible thought. If we move into Sylvia's I'll have to grow up with Eleanor and the others. Right up to when I leave home I'll be stuck with them. In my face. The whole time.

I'm back where I started.

He changes tack. 'OK, come and see the house one day when they're not there. They go to their dad's once a fortnight.'

It's not as bad as his last idea.

He's sussed that I'm cracking. 'You'll feel differently once you've seen how much better than our place it is.'

It's true, our place is a bit of a dump. We rent it so we haven't bothered to spend money on it to make it nice or anything. After Mum died Dad was too upset to stay in the house where he and Mum had lived for fifteen years, so we moved here. This place was unfurnished so we brought our own stuff.

I'm saved from answering Dad's question by a knock at the door.

'Come in.'

We both know it's Sylvia. Her smell always comes in first. I think it's hair stuff, but it might be . . . a body thing. I hated it at first, but I'm used to it now.

'Hi!' she says. Then she sits next to me and nicks one of my chips.

I forget all about what Dad and I have been talking about, because Sylvia's so kind of normal and easy to get on with. You don't have to act different when she's around.

'Yes, you may!' I grin.

'May I?' she asks, grinning back.

'Get the report done OK?' asks Dad.

That means Dad must have met Sylvia in her lunch break. They often do that.

She nods and nicks another of my chips. 'May I?' she asks with her mouth full.

'No,' I tell her, pretending to be cross.

'Sorry, Joe.' She looks at Dad. 'How was Mrs Clayton?'

Dad rolls his eyes. He works for himself, fitting gas central heating. Sylvia's talking about one of his customers.

'Still not coughing up what she owes.'

'You're too soft, Nick. You ought to tell her

you won't finish this job till she pays you for the last one.'

'Mm,' says Dad.

But we all know he won't. Sylvia's right. He *is* a soft touch.

And now he's changing the subject. So predictable. 'Nice earrings, Sylv.'

'Thanks. They're not mine. I borrowed them from Ellie.'

Something happens inside my head when she says the name Ellie. I'm remembering what Kelly Grey said, and that gets me mad again. I never thought Eleanor would come out with something like that. I thought she'd realise about Mum. That she's the only mum I'll ever have. No way am I ever having a 'brand new one'.

'I was just trying to persuade Joe to come and have a look at the house,' says Dad.

'Yes, you ought to,' says Sylvia. 'Then you can choose which bedroom you'd like.'

'Aren't you the lucky one!' says Dad, cuffing me over the head and grinning. 'That's nice of the girls to give you the choice of bedroom, isn't it?'

I don't want them being nice. It makes me feel a right baby. 'I don't care which room I have.'

I scrape my chair as I get up and I can see Dad's about to have a go at me, but Sylvia shakes her head at him and he doesn't.

I go out without saying another word and I know they'll be talking about me in a minute. I can just imagine it . . .

Oh dear. Problems, Nick? I thought Joe was OK about moving.

Don't worry, he'll be fine. He's just had to put up with bit of ribbing from his friends . . .

Huh! Adults! They don't get it!

Collect the links in the step-chain . . .

1. To see her dad, Sarah has to stay with the woman who wrecked her family. Will she do it? Find out in *One Mum Too Many!*

2. Ollie thinks a holiday with girls will be a nightmare. And it is, because he's fallen for his stepsister. Can it get any worse? Find out in *You Can't Fancy Your Stepsister*

3. Lissie's half-sister is a spoilt brat, but her mum thinks she's adorable. Can Lissie make her see what's really going on? Find out in *She's No Angel*

4. Becca's mum describes her boyfriend's daughter as perfect in every way. Can Becca bear to meet her? Find out in *Too Good To Be True*

 5. Ed's stepsisters are getting seriously on his nerves. Should he go and live with his mum? Find out in *Get Me Out Of Here*

 6. Hannah and Rachel are stepsisters. They're also best friends. What will happen to them if their parents split up? Find out in *Parents Behaving Badly*

 7. When Bethany discovers the truth about Robby, she knows her family will go ballistic. Is it possible to keep his secret from them? Find out in *Don't Tell Mum*

8. Ryan's life is made hell by his bullying stepbrother. Has he got the guts to stand up for himself? Find out in *Losing My Identity*

 9. Katie knows it's wrong to lie to her mum. Will she decide to own up, despite the consequences? Find out in *Secrets and Lies*

 11. Joe used to like Eleanor. Now, he's got to *live* with her. Can he cope? Find out in *She Wants War?*